Bird at the Window

TO KNOW TO UNDERSTAND TO PARTICIPATE
THE CANADIAN HERITAGE IS YOUR HERITAGE

**ALBERTA HERITAGE
LEARNING RESOURCES
PROJECT**

A Project of Alberta Education
Funded
By
The Alberta Heritage Savings Trust Fund
and
Dedicated to the Students
of Alberta
by the
Government of Alberta
1979

We acknowledge the co-operation
of the publishers and authors in
including their works in the Alberta Heritage collection.

MEMBERS OF THE SELECTION COMMITTEE

William F. Lockhart/*Managing Editor, Alberta Education*
Leslie L. Aitken/*Alberta Education*
Louis Burke/*Lethbridge Separate School District*
Heather-Belle Dowling/*County of Strathcona Municipal Library*
Shirley I. Paustian/*Edmonton Public School District*
Hilda Ross/*Freelancer and Instructor of Creative Writing*
John N. White/*East Smoky School Division*

David Shaw & Associates Ltd./*Project Cover Design*

Bird at the Window

JAN TRUSS

Macmillan of Canada / Toronto

ISBN   0-7705-1175-9

The Macmillan Company of Canada Limited
70 Bond Street
Toronto M5B 1X3

Printed in Canada

If I had but two loaves of bread
I would sell one and buy hyacinth
For they would feed my soul.

Bird at the Window

There! She had said it.

The moment teetered and she waited for it to fall, she like a watcher outside the window, looking in on a scene in which she was only a player, watching it like the afternoon show on television seen through the kitchen window over the yellow table past her tall mother peeling red apples, through the cloud of cigarette smoke over her father's greasy-armed old armchair, through all the windows of the afternoon community where everyone is watching the same soap opera on television because it is still snowing outside, soddening the flat fields.

His smile hung trapped, caught in the tease of her swinging legs, smooth and long in cinnamon panty-hose, neat, right up and under the little edge of her light tweed skirt.

Until this moment she hadn't admitted it, hadn't given it words even in the night or on waking, not even to herself. And the words were only an impulse now. She had not intended to tell Mr. Olson—although, who else was there to test a problem against who would neither preach nor fly off the handle? Preaching would be unbearable. It was just that she had been passing his classroom and looked in to see him sitting there alone, bent over the exercise books and papers on his table. Sensing her there, he had looked up and smiled, smiled the way he did, wise and kind and mocking all at the same time, and she had gone in and sat on top of a front desk—blurted it out, words coming cold out of the nag of her fear. She had said it—then it was quiet.

The empty desks seemed to breathe, heavy brown presences behind her, and the noises of school crept into the long pause.

1

Mr. Olson put down his red marking pencil, pushed the pile of his marking aside, and sat rubbing a finger up and down the greying bristles where his beard and sideburns met. Why me? Oh, dear God, why this one? What now was he supposed to say?

She had said it and it sounded so matter of fact. Just a dry statement. She had said it and neither had the sky fallen nor the world come to an end. The monotonous voice went on lecturing in the room across the hallway; footsteps shuffled down the corridor and a locker door slammed tinnily. The heating system choked into a new spasm of life. A bird whimpered under the eavestroughing outside the window, and Angela Moynahan, the brain, sat on top of a front-row desk twisting a long length of pale hair round her wrist—waiting.

The teacher watched her pale eyes watching the thin bits of snow whip past the bars of the classroom window. He saw the flakes crash and disappear into the muddied gravel road. A few thin trees, out there, planted in Centennial year, were trying to break into bud.

"You could have an abortion," he made himself say, tentative, awkward, but gentle. Then he looked down again at the work on his desk, put a swift check mark at the bottom of a neat page. Being so personal was like raping her confidence. He was uncomfortable.

She stopped twisting her hair and sat on her hands. "It's snowing. Again," she said dejectedly, giving his words time to ease themselves down into the morass of her panic. "Snow. Again. Winter seems forever."

He glanced through the pages of the next exercise book but looked up to persist diffidently, "It does happen, you know. Young women do these days. You don't have to be . . ." He didn't know what word to use. He smiled doubtfully and submitted "detoured". "You don't have to be detoured from your intentions, unless you want to be, of course."

She let her legs swing, heard the school-sound hollow down the long corridor, felt the hot familiarity of the old classroom and at the same time felt it was unreal, all of it. But she had made THE THING real. Said it out loud. And the panic inside was real. And he had said . . . abortion. Abortion. Not a catchword on a Women's Lib banner on television, or an article in her mother's *Chatelaine*. Not an academic discussion in a dangerously liberal class. No. Abortion—personal. Real. Bloody. A wrench between the legs, for her, Angela Moynahan. She crossed her legs.

A bird thudded against the window, fluttered, regained itself, and flew off into the whip of the thin snow.

She shuddered. "It's like a prison, this room, this school," she complained and swept the green and brown faded drabness with a look of both defiance and despair. "Why do they never paint it? This room, ever since I came into it, always there's been a bird outside the bars. Sometimes singing. For three years, ever since I first came in for literature, I've sat and wondered, is the bird shut out or are we shut in? There's always a bird in that corner under the roof. Do you notice?" she asked him urgently, making him look at her.

He smiled, surprised as he always was for a moment again by the blondness of her. The palest, most shockingly white eyes he had ever seen. Must have come from some Scandinavian ancestor. Like porcelain. A constant surprise. He wondered if a high-school girl knows she is beautiful. Does anyone ever tell her?

"Of course I notice." He met her gaze gently and waited for what she had to say.

She sat on her hands, hunched her shoulders and leaned forward, looking at him directly. "Is that what you would say to your daughter?" she asked him roughly.

He almost retorted that it hadn't happened to his daughter but he stopped himself. Too small an answer. He looked away from her question but tried not to avoid the demand of her intellect. He looked across the rows of brown desks to remember the girl who had been his daughter. "Yes it is. Yes—" Then he looked past her face to the snow again, suddenly resenting the despair of winter prolonged. The girl watched him, quizzing him, half mocking with her young ferocity. It's the golden skin makes the eyes so pale, even in winter, he thought.

"But Angela!" His words came now. "Angela, what about your summer, your year in Europe? I thought you had it all settled, planned —?"

She frowned and for an instant was nonplussed, then collected herself. He saw the guards go up.

"Well, my work permits came," she said, lifting her chin defiantly as though he was the one raising obstacles. "And, well, even if — well, pregnancy's not a disease, is it?" she fought him.

He shrugged, accepting her swerve to hostility with practised tolerance. "No, there's nothing to stop you, I guess." Inwardly he mocked his own thoughts, his other-age visions of golden girls with butterfly eyes by summer cathedrals, and with some asperity went on, "It's just that I find it less than romantic to think of your hard-earned summer weighed down with a big belly." He made a sad little gesture with his shoulders and returned to his marking.

She pressed her hands into her hard waist and snorted, angry at herself for the tears that came. A bird cried outside the window. They both looked towards the cry and saw each other look.

"I'm sorry, Angela. That wasn't kind. But the way I feel." He looked at her lean jaw and wide eyes, the flat belly and the heavy mass of straight pale hair, and twisted his face wryly, sighing, "Oh, I suppose it's just part of the teacher's job to want to see the bars come down for some of you." He looked at the window. "I think I could quote you, couldn't I, your own words," he pointed towards the assignments he was marking, " 'send out swans to wing wildly and butterflies to dance for more than one springtime'."

She flushed. "But I've blown it," she said and hung her head, self-conscious at having her work quoted. You gave him your fragile ideas and he held them so seriously. "I'm sorry," she admitted, off guard to herself because of his caring. "I've blown it," she repeated. "You must get discouraged. I'm sorry," she said again and frowned. "It was me caged in—is me—"

"Oh come on," he urged her, less reticent because her need had shown through. "Angela, do something about it!" But he shouldn't be encouraging a student like this. He was running right into the blind wall of community condemnation even by letting her talk. She shouldn't be talking to him about it.

"What about your mother, Angela?"

The girl sucked her cheeks in and looked through him with dead eyes.

"What's your mother's attitude going to be?" He wondered

about the tall, vague woman he had met the one time he had been to the house to drop off a book that Angela had wanted. It had been the end of the summer holiday and he'd been amazed at the lavish flower garden persuaded to such blossoming out of the prairie's short summer, surprised too by the strange rich colours inside the small farmhouse. Previously he had only known that somebody stitched exquisite clothes for an only daughter.

"I shall never tell my mother." The reply was flat. "Nor my father. I wouldn't tell them."

"Then it's going to be difficult, isn't it?"

The dead eyes surveyed him, unsmiling. "I'm not telling anybody." She heard a wildness in her voice and watched him turn back to his marking because she'd left him nothing to say. "You're the only one I've told. Sorry. I don't know why I told you. It's pointless," she ended sounding belligerent.

"Safety valve," he offered, not looking up. "But you must have a partner in this, eh? Sorry. None of my business." He paused and she watched his pencil lingering over a page of close writing. He put an extra-long check mark and scribbled "Excellent" under it. Somebody would fly high on that. She looked wearily at the battered exercise books with their searchings and secrets inside, pages where kids had dared be poets and passionate and crazy romantic—to flutter out of their cages, briefly. "But Angela," he went on and looked at her steadily, "You will finish school, won't you?" he asked her quietly.

She turned her mouth down and raised her eyes to the ceiling, "Oh sure, sir, I'll finish. That really is the only thing that matters in this community, next to putting on a shower, isn't it? Things we understand!" He heard her snideness and refused to take up the quarrel, to haggle over the entrenched community values. He went on marking. She picked up her books as though to leave, then changed her mind.

"Yes, I shall finish. It's seven weeks to the end and by then I shall be two and a half months—pregnant." She forced the last word out, a boldness.

"Good Lord, child, you can't even know for sure." He stood up and towered over her. "You silly child, go and talk to the school nurse—the doctor—somebody."

She tossed her hair insolently, giving him an urge to slap her.

Schoolgirl reactions for hiding embarrassment irritated him. He spoke curtly, impatient with her, "Well, go and do something about it. Even if you are. . . . So soon. Well, you could hardly call it an abortion. For Christ's sake go and talk to the nurse today—now."

"No," she spat. "This is my business. Not for local gossip."

"Then go to your family doctor."

"No."

"Oh, don't be silly." But he already knew that a family doctor would be too personal. "It's just his job, Angela. He wouldn't moralize."

"No. *No*, Mr. Olson. I think he would have to get my mother's permission. Anyhow, I wouldn't want him to know. Sort of corny, I guess. But, no. I couldn't."

He still felt he had to urge her. "Young woman, stop being so silly. Seventeen is too soon to have messed up your—one little life."

"Eighteen," she snapped.

"Seventeen or eighteen, dammit," he snapped back, "it's time to take yourself to a doctor in Calgary; look out for yourself a bit." But even as the words flew he knew that it was not so easy when you were seventy miles away from the anonymity of the city and without a car. Even space makes prisoners. Good Lord, how far should he get himself mixed up in this? "I have a friend, a doctor; I could arrange it," he committed himself.

"No. No," she hissed. "No, no, NO." She could see herself splayed on a narrow white table, bared, being probed, and she flushed, impotent against an onrush of humiliation. She tossed her hair back but he saw the tears ready to brim and he turned away, looked out of the window through the thin driving snow across the small town splattered on the big grey landscape, looked past the five elevators to the grey weight of the leaden prairie sky.

"You're being melodramatic, Angela." He said it mildly. "Just grow up. This is your one, your only little life." He heard her breathe in sharply behind him. "Anyway, you're probably meeting trouble that doesn't exist," he goaded her, wondering how much of the silly little girl still lingered in that cool scholar's mind he thought of as Angela. He squinted his eyes to look into the emptiness of the horizonless sky and found nothing.

6

"You're not fair," she choked, and steadied her dignity with a lift of the head. "I am not being melodramatic. And I am not going to tell my mother. And I am not going to get an abortion. And I would never get a baby adopted."

He let the outpouring fall on his back. She heard her words and knew they were the words you said when it hadn't happened to you. He watched a woman in curlers holding her coat together hurrying past the Centennial trees towards Main Street. Let bright Angela's words run on, the brave morality of the young. He had heard it all before.

"And I will not tell my mother ever." She paused, then finished flat. "And I am not going to marry Gordy."

He turned now and winced at the tears on her cheeks. Oh dear God, if this were my daughter! He wanted to put his arms about her, save her, let the spirit stay proud. Instead he said sharply, "Don't get hysterical, child. Gordon Kopec?" He raised his eyebrows; knew he was right. "Poor Gordon," he said quietly. "You should have known better." He sat down behind the pile of books again and looked incredulously, hopelessly at the girl, so vivid, so lovely. He remembered the pale clod of a heavy boy-man who had slipped away from school to work around the farms, more than three years ago.

"Oh, don't you worry about Gordy," she flashed. "Poor Gordon! I'm not going to let him marry me."

The automatic time buzzer razed through the corridors cutting her off, ended the period.

"You wouldn't tell—I'm sorry," she frowned, looking down at his marking, but before he had time to answer the next class was filtering in, moaning about the snow. He watched her swing her tidy little behind and shake her heavy hair free as she pushed through the incoming crowd.

He sighed, teacher weary. Damn, damn, damn Gordon Kopec. Nobody Gordon. She'll marry him and he won't have the brains to know what he's got. Committed with their bodies, they always end up marrying—these serious girls.

7

Fifteen, fourteen, even ten days ago she had run up the driveway home singing, leaping, caught in a dream. So this was love. Tomorrow, oh tomorrow, he will sit against me, ask me out somewhere, put his hand on mine. Their glances kept catching each other across the classroom, and she, Angela, was vulnerable like all the other girls, blushing and silly with love.

Tomorrow he will ask me. And tomorrow it will come right. It can't happen to me, not now. My back is aching. Please God, make it right today. Today make him ask me.

But today she had made that thing real; told Mr. Olson.

It was still snowing at the end of the day; thin wet snow lashing at the students as they made a dash for the line-up of engine-running school vans. "Some summer!" high-schoolers grumbled as they filled up the back places on the icy leather seats, shaking the wet off their books and wiping their faces; shivering.

"Hey—no heat back here, Art!" one of the guys yelled across the rabble of the little kids and over the blurred racket of the radio Art Kopec kept on loud to drown out the noise.

"Hey—Art—it's freezing back here," other voices yelled at the humped back of the driver till he sagged round in his seat. Art Kopec pushed his red hunting cap back on his raw new crewcut, bulged belligerent hostility with watery eyes from his big bald face towards the complaints at the back. Art Kopec. Gordon's uncle. His father's brother. Angela shuddered, turned up the white fur of her collar and pushed her chin down into its softness, breathing warm damp into it. She pulled her coat together over her thighs, trying to hold it closed with the weight of her homework books. She turned away towards the snow at the window, squeezing her knees together in mute revulsion against kinship with Gordy Kopec's Uncle Art.

Uncle Art was waddling down the aisle of the van. He kicked peevishly at a second-grader's yellow lunch pail, yelling treble at the little kids not to eat in his van. He wasn't going to pick up no filth after no kids!

The radio revved and blurred violently, crashed into Angela, thickening her panic, panic gnawing through the cold, nagging the noise, shredding in her throat and her chest and her thighs. Art Kopec stopped in the aisle two seats in front of her. She saw in the pale, fat face the baby he must have been. Baby. Slob. Fat baby.

"And what are you smart alecs griping about now?" his whine trembled hysterically at the guys.

"Oh, come on, Art, you must know it's killing back here," all the shivering thin six-foot-four of Harold Boon tried to reason.

"You should have had to start this crate when I did. That'd learn ya. Then you'd have thought you was cold," the baby face blustered.

"You're paid to do something about it," somebody spoke up.

"If you guys don't like it, git off an' walk. Make men of some of you longhairs."

"Daaaaaaaaa," the guys moaned together and the rest of the bus took it up into a howl of insolence that met Damion Good as he thrust out of the wind into the bus. He stood on the steps with his long hair blown, wet and black, and his weathered face laughing.

"Well, thanks a lot," he bowed, "and the same to the lot of you. Great to be welcomed."

"Dam Good. Dam Good," the junior high kids chanted dangerously as Art Kopec waddled back down the bus with his neck spreading purple over the red check of his jacket. Damion Good waited for him with an excess of polite attention, then bowed the fat man to his seat.

"You can drive away now, sweetie. I'm the last girl you were waiting for." He shook his curls forward and simpered through everybody's giggles towards the back of the bus.

Angela pushed her face down deeper into the white fur and blushed. Crazy to travel twelve years on a school van with the same guys and then one day catch glances that make you shy. But then she was shy, not easy with small talk. And none of them had really treated her as a date-likely girl—only as the brain. She frowned at her own confusion.

9

Today, this crazy day, she had said it and made it real, told Mr. Olson. Today, crazy irony, Damion Good was going to sit by her, ask her, admit to the reel of those glances across the classrooms. She knew he would; today. But why only now? Resentment for the unfairness of things, pity for herself, poor trapped thing, overwhelmed her and she bit her lip, mad at the tears she felt for herself. She ached inside, tired and confused by her own confusion. Why should it matter anyhow—it was hard to make words for it—that Gordy Kopec had put his penis into her. There! She'd thought the words. Poor Gordy! Was she changed? Did it show that she had done—that thing? Even the fear—no, no—NO—not a baby. A late clot of blood. Nothing— except a fear in her.

She smiled through the white fur at Damion because his eyes were smiling at her.

And everybody talks as though abortion is . . . easy—talks as though. . . .

"Oh-ho, Angelar, what big eyes you have." Silly, fooling, easy words to make a noncommittal contact, safe against rejection. Make her seem less formidable. "Did anyone ever tell you you look like the queen of the Siamese cats?"

"Ooh, often. Purr purr," she caught the invitation of his banter while he draped himself beside her with his long arm across the back of the seat. Then the bus jerked into gear and his books slid under the seat by her feet. She tried not to laugh.

"Oh well, so much for my luck," he shrugged, and foraged under the seat to dump his muddied books on her lap on top of hers. "Just when I was aiming to make a good impression." Say the truth out loud like a joke and the embarrassment's gone. People laugh. They really think you're a joker. But this girl gives him a shrewd look from under her summer eyelashes, a quick lit-up look. How does she look like summer when there's only been winter? He puts his arm back along the seat.

"A Dam Good impression, how else?" she quips, but he hears a caress and moves in closer.

There is mud streaked across his fingers. A long brown sensitive hand. Not like Gordy's pale pudgy one.

She shuddered and pulled her coat tighter under the books on her thighs. "It's so cold," she shivered and wished the heaviness of her misery-fear would lift and let her lean easily into this guy's soft parka and laugh and tease and fly high, and be light and silly with love.

They pushed their knees together for warmth and his arm was across her shoulders. "Never mind," he said, "only thirty-four schooldays left—and it could be summer, next week perhaps—maybe tomorrow."

She shuddered. Thirty-four schooldays. Forty-eight my days to get through, to decide what to do. Got to do something. Panic seeps in her throat again and she leans hard against his arm. But it has to come right now that she has tempted fate, broken the spell, and told Mr. Olson. Hasn't she known since childhood that if you expect the most terrible thing to happen it never does. That day, the end of the summer before last, if she'd expected, or been prepared, or said the words that her little brother could get drowned, then it would never have happened. But she'd never even thought the words, just set a place for him at the supper table—unprepared. So it had happened.

"And twenty-four days to exams. If I work, which I might, I could beat you to the scholarship. It's the cash I'm after."

"And I suppose you think I don't need it," she started with vehemence, then trailed off, snagging on the implications.

"Aw come on, woman! You can just be a dumb and beautiful blonde, get married and live happily ever after." He nudged her with his knee.

What does he know? Suspicion sickened through her. "Thanks," she said, "thanks for nothing." She turned from him and wiped a hole in the steam on the window. Snow streaked cold across the flat fields.

She watched the family of small children the bus was letting off, watched them start the long trudge up the bleak mud-slimed road, their big winter overshoes flapping, not done up, their coats blown into their pushed bodies. Dots of humanity carrying bright lunch pails across the blowing monotony. Snow was beginning to stick again; grey streaks on the dun earth. Two brown ducks sat on the slough's ripples by the roadside. And her back ached.

But Damion was warm against her. She leaned back into him. "My feet are freezing," she said and spread her ankles close to

11

his legs. "Oh, you could probably beat me," she shrugged as though she didn't care, "if you could ever be secure enough to be serious—in your school work I mean. Or if you were a girl. We work, you know."

"I'm glad I'm not," he said and he saw a cold response crimp her lips. He put his hand over hers ostentatiously to keep his options open. This girl backs off, turns off. He stretched his fingers over hers trying to be close but not vulnerable. Where was he going wrong?

In a sudden sag into unreasonableness she hated him. How easy to be male. Not let down. Not eliminated by your own body. Shrivelling herself against the cold glass of the window she pulled away from him, rubbed at the steam with her bare hand. Kids on the other side of the van screamed into laughter, cheeky little guys. They had drawn a heart in the steam with D.G. and A.M. in it and drawn wings and a halo. "A damn good Angel," they shouted to tease across the bus.

"Cut that out," Art Kopec screamed, watching it all in his mirror.

Damion shook his fist good-naturedly. "You just wait, Charlie Finn and Jackie Hogan. I'll cream the two of ya."

Angela blushed and looked away into the snow drifting. So, it shows. Angela M. loves Damion G. Damion loves Angela. It shows and it hurts. The noise ground into her; wheels on gravel and gravel flying; super-happy disc jockey half tuned out; kids raising their yells louder to cover the radio's fuzz. Thirty-four more days of riding the school van, to the end she's counted for, and now she's wishing this one drive home would freeze, hang suspended and innocent for ever. If she turns towards Damion their eyes admit and she'll have to look away to catch her feelings as they sway. Was there ever a beginning with Gordy? She had ridden the bus with him on her first day at school. She can still remember the leather engine-warm September smell of it, and Gordy's grandfather, the driver then, till that weekend he was drowned with her brother.

The damp clothes are warming up and somebody has peeled an orange. The school bus smells of little kids and oranges and banana peels pitched under seats. Harold Boon talks to Damion from the seat behind, making him turn over his shoulder. Her back aches. Harold Boon is saying that he won't be in school tomorrow because he has to drive his mother into hospital in Calgary to see a specialist. So easy. Easy just to catch a ride with them. But what excuse could she make? To her mother? To Mrs. Boon?

"Roads'll be bad," they say and they all look across the sodden land. Damion leans across her and clears a bigger hole in the window steam. They are passing the Kopec place, a bare two-storey unpainted house at the end of a straight path, like a small child's drawing, a house on a straight stem. Not a tree though. A drawing in faint pencil-crayon brown. The yard is mud between the unpainted house and the unpainted barns and the ramshackle chicken-houses. Gordy's old black truck, a '59 G.M., is parked in the mud by the house.

"You and Gord going to the wedding dance at Beupeur, Ange?" Harold Boon prods her shoulder to ask, so she has to half turn to answer. Her chin touches Damion's hand and her breath catches.

"No," she said, not knowing she had made that decision till she heard that "No".

"Looks like his truck's stuck so he won't be going nowhere nohow," Damion volunteered with sarcasm and his fingers pressed into her shoulder. She tries not to react but stare instead at Art Kopec's bulging neck. She hates, hates that truck parked there in the black rutted mud.

"Hey Angela. Come with me?" He had said it.

"Why?" She faced him sharply. Silly thing to say, but her edginess has cut her composure. Why, why, why? Had somebody told him, "Yes she does. A good lay"? But no. She sees bewilderment briefly in his eyes before he catches himself and puts on his clowning. He pulled his arm from behind her and cupped his face in his hands mock tragically.

"Christ, O Christo!" he moaned. "I work up to it. I gather courage. O Christo! That'll teach me to ask the school brain for a date! Why? it says." He rattled on while she looked out of the window biting her lip. "I know, Miss Socrates, the unconsidered date would not be worth the dating."

She turned with her head on one side and tried to look calculating and cool, smooth and choosy. "Okay," she said, "it's

13

a date." Then she was shy again and began to pull on her gloves and shuffle her books, standing up to get off the van. "Seeya," she said and pushed past him. He moved over to her window seat to sit on her warmth and to smile without subterfuge through the hole in the steam on the window down into her smile where she stood backed into the wind waiting for the van to pull away before she picked up the mail from the roadside mailbox and put the letters in between the books in her arms. She turned across the wind into the long curve of the Moynahan driveway between the trees her mother had planted.

The white board house with the red shingled roof is set in trees, wind-pushed evergreens thickening among the just-budding poplars and the spiky tracery of caragana hedges. "I just had to plant trees," Dinah Moynahan always explains. "It was so unprotected when we built it."

"What about your mother?" Mr. Olson had said.

Mr. Olson, how could I tell my mother? If it were somebody else, not me, she would say, "Such a pity," mildly. But it is me, it is *me*. . . The door is painted bright red, right into the kitchen where the coffee is waiting welcome in the enamelled orange pot on a low burner. Coffee smell and red apples. Home.

"Hi Angela," Dinah called from the sitting-room extension that had been the luxury addition to the house, added, together with a bathroom, after harvest last year.

Angela kicked her muddy boots behind the white painted drawers with the vines on top reaching up to hooks in the ceiling, drawers her mother had dragged there two feet in front of the coat-hooks on the wall by the door when no porch, no entranceway, ever seemed to be forthcoming. "So we can eat without looking at old coats and dirty boots," Dinah had said, and twisted the vines round binder twine.

Angela dumped her coat on the white-painted old kitchen chair, her books by the apples on the yellow table, poured two brown mugs of coffee and took them with the mail to the new room where the long windows look through thin places in the sheltering trees to the bleak windblow of the flat fields. She put the coffee on the arm of the long floral-covered bright chesterfield where her mother sat with her legs tucked up and her head on one side, critically watching the stitches as her fingers

14

smocked a length of soft turquoise printed cloth. Her hair was slipping out of its loose bun at the back, pale spirals hanging. Five purple hyacinths in a low earthen pot on the wide window ledge crowded the room with their perfume. There were sewing things and bright cloth everywhere.

"Well, at last I'm making a start on your travelling things," Dinah said, holding up the smocking for Angela to see. "Isn't that effective?" There was a lot of Midland England left in her accent, a rough edge on the refinement.

Angela sat back in the small armchair now and turned away from the blowing view towards her mother and the solid blue wall behind the chesterfield where one of Dinah's large tapestry-creations rioted across the wall like a tease of a medieval church hanging. It was an art form of cloth and embroidery and beads depicting angels as heralds with long trumpets rousing a flurry of jewelled birds from bending branches. A wild, extravagant thing, flamboyant.

"I love smocking. I'm glad it's in fashion again," Dinah said, still holding up the turquoise work.

"It's beautiful, Mum. But all that work!"

"I don't mind that. Although everybody is going to look pregnant this year."

Angela looked at her mother sharply. Does she suspect? No. Suppose she just said now, "But Mum I am"? But she didn't say it.

"What's my mother got to say? You open her letter."

Angela slit the blue airletter with the blade of her mother's scissors. "She says she's getting your old room ready for me. She's bought a new mattress for your old bed. She says I can have a job for the summer in the bakery up the street, a job in the shop behind the counter, and I'm to let her know quick if I want it. It's just for July and August."

Dinah frowned over the smocking. "Well, I have reservations. But I suppose it could be all right for two months if you want to do it. And if you save the money, then take off for Spain or Crete, somewhere exotic, it might be worth it. At least I'll envy you that part when we're stuck here in winter."

It was so easy to let herself be soothed by the normality of home and kid herself that everything was adventure and easy as it was two months ago, three weeks ago. Angela sipped her black coffee and pushed back hard into the pressure of a humped cushion. "I hope Dad can do without me. You don't want to get back to chores again, do you?"

"If it gets too much for him, I imagine Gordon can come and live in a bit. There really isn't that much to be done over at Kopec's. Your Dad likes having Gordon around—although I sometimes think you see too much of him." The afterthought came out serenely but Angela's insides quaked. She stared down at her grandmother's blue airletter. Why didn't she say as she had said to Mr. Olson, "I am pregnant"? She studied her mother soothingly smocking, so serene.

"Claire Froman's getting married on Saturday. I'm going to the wedding dance over a Beupeur Hall. Okay Mum? I'm going with Damion Good."

"With Damion! That's nice. He's filled out this year, hasn't he? Poor Claire. Silly girl to get herself tied down so soon."

Angela watched her mother interspersing her words with stitches and she pushed her back harder into the hump of the cushion. "Maybe Claire should have got an abortion." She said the words bright and brittle, got up as she said them to wind up a reel of red thread that had rolled under the sewing machine treadle. She wound the thread in, waiting for her mother's re-action. Why didn't she say just as brightly, "Mother, maybe I should get an abortion," say it with her back turned. Dinah's silence hung in the scent of the hyacinths against the wind at the windows and Angela nipped the end of the thread into the crack in the spool and set it with the rest of the spooled colours in the tin box that had once held finest English assorted biscuits.

"Thanks Angela."

That was all she said.

Angela wanted to stamp her foot like a frustrated child, make her mother tell what was going on in that elegant head. She had married young, very young, hadn't she? She was only thirty-seven now. "Mother," she started to say. "Mum . . ." She put her face down into the hyacinth flowers.

"Ummm?" Fingers still stitching, uninterrupted.

"Oh nothing. I love the way these smell."

"Like bluebells, English bluebells. They don't grow here."

16

The haze in her mother's voice made Angela turn and ask, "Don't you ever regret leaving it all behind, settling here? Don't you miss things?"

Dinah paused between stitches, gave a funny little smile. "You be a judge of that when you've worked your two months in the streets where I grew up. But yes, of course there are things. I have been homesick—for country lanes and a bike, and bluebells in bunches to take home on the handlebars. When your job finishes you should get a bike and do a September tour of the little lanes of England before you take off."

Angela crashed into her own thoughts. She picked up a pattern envelope. The pregnant smocked look. In September she might have a big belly—if . . .

She made a dash for the new deep blue bathroom, turned on the taps to confuse her noises, punched her hard fists into her flat cold stomach, heaved it in and out, sat on the ivory lavatory seat, and punched and punched and heaved inside.

Maybe she's wrong. Maybe she is not pregnant. In the black hours of nights that wouldn't go to sleep she reasoned and relived and unreasoned again, tossing from memory to panic to despair and back into hope. Maybe she was just run down and subconsciously keyed up about the coming exams. Maybe the months of tension between herself and her father had taken their toll. He had been so against her travelling, hostile to the very idea of his daughter not going directly from school to university.

It was Gordon Kopec who had taken her beer bottles to the depot to collect the thirty cents a dozen that over three years had amounted to a hundred and twenty-nine dollars in her savings account. She had combed the ditches and the lakeside to salvage beer bottles tossed out of cars and trucks or left in piles by week-end fishermen and hunters. Her father said it was degrading, but she hadn't cared about that. The motive of her year in Europe had been enough.

"The things some people will do for their damn-fool high-falutin ideas," Joe Moynahan had berated her. "A girl with your brains should be a credit to her family, not turn herself into a tramp so she can go hitch-hiking."

"Get everything ready; he'll come round, you'll see," Dinah had promised while Angela fumed and pondered, wondering how two such different people as her mother and father had come to-gether and tolerated each other through years of farm isolation. Although—they had seemed like a family when Rory was still alive. Since his funeral they only ever seemed remotely together when they watched the same program on television in the warmth of the kitchen where the old black and white set kept its place with Joe Moynahan's faded, fat pink plush armchair. He never had taken to the new room that had replaced Rory's porch-bedroom. . . . In the tossing night, Angela remembers flashes of scenes in detail.

18

Dinah and Angela watching the program on ancient civilizations from hard chairs at the yellow table.

"I'd really love to get as far as Crete," Angela said and Joe exploded, "Bloody big ideas for a poor farmer's daughter. It's that teacher, that Olson, filling country kids' heads with ideas beyond their stations. It's time somebody got rid of him. He's no good for ordinary folk the likes of us. Him and his highfalutin' ideas."

"Oh, Dad," she had sighed impatiently. "Dad, there are kids from everywhere travelling round Europe now." And then she had changed her tones to wheedle him, "Dad, me old dear, you travelled. You came here. See, it runs in the family."

"That was different. I came to work, to make a living. Bit different from the long-haired scum on the roads these days."

"Oh Dad!" She had wanted to humour her father's bigotry, make him see. "Mum travelled, didn't you, Mum? She came by herself when she was no older than I am now."

Dinah had looked up momentarily from the blue shirt elbow she was patching and had smiled vaguely.

"That was different. Your mother wasn't roaming the roads. She came to stay with decent, God-fearing folk."

"Yes," Dinah had interjected gently, "the Bennets seemed like relatives. They had written to my Mum and Dad ever since my brother had done his air training here. He wasn't much older than you when he came. The Bennets' son, Kane, had been lost over Germany too, you know, same raid as Chris. And the war still seemed so close when I came in '53."

"Then you never went back home. I bet your parents wondered if the Bennets were so good when they let you marry Dad, just like that." What had made her say that? It was out of place. She tempered it lamely, "It must have been a shock to them, Mum," and Dinah had countered with a laugh, staccato. "My poor mother. She'll never forgive me. Poor Mum. But it was Canada, too, to blame. My big brother had filled my head with it; said he was coming to settle here after the war. I came instead," said with finality.

Suddenly wanting to be conciliatory, Angela had asked, "Would you be happier, Dad, if I stayed a bit with Mum's poor

Mum? She's always writing to say how much she wants me to go and stay."

Dinah had put her sewing down, had started to say something, then thought better of it.

"Sounds like a better idea than starting off tramping the roads with God knows what trash," Joe had said. It was his truce statement. He reckoned by doing that, she would have enough cash left to travel decently and pay her way in decent hotels.

Through the night Angela could live again the old scenes, then crash into the present, "Please God, make it come right. Please make it come right before the wedding dance. Let me start afresh with Damion. Please."

All week, in the nights, she put on the bedside lamp, bent its coiled neck to spot the light low so her mother, so nobody would see it under the door. She read, made herself work at her homework, anything to escape from a mind that couldn't lie down. If the rest of the house slept, she made futile visits to the dark bathroom, straining, trying everything, sick in the fear that her mother, or somebody, would hear her and know. Her back ached. A hope. She sat or lay for anguished hours with her hands pressed into the ache of her groins. She wrote assignments that in the night seemed profound as she fitted philosophy to the nagging thoughts of her experience. "Nothing happens except it happens deep in the lonely mind," she wrote for Mr. Olson as she tussled with the nothing, the emptiness, the void, that had barbed her to Gordon, and reeled again at remembered glances caught across a room from Damion, glances that made her look away, reeling. From remembering she quaked back into her own fear, fear spawned out of the nothing she had done with Gordon. "Activity is merely a non-happening, a non-experience, until it touches the secret places where the mind flutters solitary," she wrote, and made herself remember ruthlessly the clumsy couplings half on, half off the torn and stuffing-spilling seat of the '59 truck with its cold stranger of a steering column nudging the indignity. Where had she been then? Reeling? No. NO. She had taken off while that thing was happening, chasing her roaming mind, even working out math problems while poor Gordy had gasped and pushed and pressed into her, doing what he had to do. Poor Gordon. Even now, her panic could not fit itself to Gordon. He had never touched her— not as much as a glance from Damion had. Just the anticipation of Damion coming to pick her up on Saturday night was already a quickness in the secret places of her mind. "Experience exists only as it is felt and formulated in a mind alone, lonely," she wrote, thoughts coming because Damion was happening and Gordon . . .

Gordy had just been there, a periphery sociability like community bingo, and bridal showers, and Sunday morning church. And she had just let him be there to disguise her aloneness so she could move acceptably in the closed togetherness of the small community. He had always been there, and not to accept him would have seemed a pettiness. To reject Gordy, poor Gordy, seemed like a dirty trick.

It had been like that when she stood up from the supper table to answer his phone call, playing with the cord, her parents behind her still eating.

"No. No, Gordy. No." She said it gently, frowning out of the window. The cattle were standing in a huddle. More snow. More snow. In May—more snow!

"No. Honest Gordy. I'd rather not."

Such a long pause. Then he said the snow was coming down again. Looks bad. Holding up seeding. But, oh, come on, she can't have that much homework that she can't take Saturday night off.

"Gordy. I didn't say that was the reason. I am going to the dance."

Through the leafless caragana she had watched a truck sloshing the road up. The pause seemed for miles.

"Gordy. I'm going with Damion Good."

Behind her Joe Moynahan had grunted disapproval and she had heard Gordon's breath whistle in the phone. Her horse galloped side-on to the wind, down the fence-line with the neighbour's horses.

"We're in the middle of supper, Gord. Yes, I'll tell Dad you'll be around, sure. Seeya Gordy."

"So now you're taking up with fancypants Good, are you?"
her father had sneered as she sat down. "Watch out for the likes
of him. Big Farmer's high-and-mighty sons!"

Angela had picked at her supper, pushed her back into the
sharp spindles of the old kitchen chair. She felt mean. Poor
Gordy. Would he take somebody else? As far as she knew he
had never taken any other girl out.

The rest of the week he was there for supper because he
was helping with chores and her father invited him. She had
looked at him across the bright bowls of food and seen a
stranger. Was marriage like that? She watched her mother so
separate from her father, ruminating somewhere she kept for
herself. They used to joke about her private world when Rory
was there. Then, he would snap his fingers in front of her nose
and say, "Come back, Mum," and they'd all laugh, her Dad too.
But did her mother and her father make anything happen, really
happen, each in the other?

Gordon across the table chewing next to her father; sometimes he looked at her. Nothing happened. It was hard to believe
they'd ever touched, ever done that thing. The sweat, the hot
skin, the wordless fumbling to roll a crackling safe onto his
risen thing in the dark parked truck while she waited, and the
cool synthetic impact of it—all only the little facts of memory
—the odour of genitals stronger than his sweat in the warm cab
and afterwards the pulling up and pushing down of clothing
before he spoke the one question, "Okay?", then put the headlights on and drove away. All just the little facts of memory,
dismembered from herself. It was nothing. Nothing. No more
personal than her putting her hand, her arm up a cow to turn
a calf with him watching, or putting piglets to suck. He was just
Gordy, who in the habits of the years had become an extension
of the family, fitting himself in as he had fitted himself into her,
accepting hospitality without comment, as his due, without
mention. To do that thing and never give it words, never
mention it, made it as though it had never happened.

But across the table he was alien, alien against her nut-brown
father with the flecked brown eyes and the fringe of white
bristles round the edge of his head. Gordon was pale, a blur like

22

a little kid's runny painting; baby pink with spiky baby hair, snipped short.

"None of that hippy stuff about Gordon," her father said often. "A good clean guy, with no funny ideas."

Gordon fit in with her father; two old men mumbling on the other side of the table about trucks and pigs and seeding and who was selling out. Always what. Never why? Buddies. Gordon chewing, talking, untroubled, while she, Angela, sucked and pushed at the ache in her back, and snagged in the hooks of her fear.

Resentment hurt her, resentment for the hurt—to her "one little life", as Mr. Olson would say. Ugly, not fun, not crazy fun making out in a truck. Ugly. Beating herself with her frantic fists in the school toilets, jumping hard down too many stairs, reaching desperate and too high, straining with the massive weights of too many bales and bags of feed, blasting herself with all her father's purgatives from the medicine cupboard in the new bathroom; flagellating herself while he went about his man's work untroubled. But it wasn't any business of his. He wasn't any business of hers, was he? And yet, poor Gordon, he wouldn't hurt anyone, not anything.

If she could bring herself to cry he would stroke her hair and caress her like a kitten, as he had at the end of the day of her brother's funeral, his grandfather's funeral too.

While neighbours had mourned and murmured in the kitchen she had gone to sit on the cot in the narrow porch that was Rory's bedroom, his own den, the little porch meant to be the house entrance but no one had ever put any steps under the high door. A door too high off the ground hanging unused. It was after she had piled up Rory's schoolbooks to take back, and taken the crumpled tissues from under his pillow, Gordon standing there watching—it was the tissues that did it—that she had finally cried.

It was then that Gordon had first put his arms about her and stroked her bare arms and her long thighs, and kissed the tears on her eyes. She had pushed her face into his warm neck and clung to him. He had seemed so much older then, twenty to her sixteen, so calm, so sensible, so in charge.

She watched him across the supper table piling his plate with a second heaped meal, deliberately mashing the earthy potatoes her mother had cooked in their red-brown skins. He wouldn't eat the skins. He would leave them for her to pick off the side of his plate. Always he mashed his food up, like baby food. Pap. She stared at the stranger across the table. Pale pink Gordy, easy and at home, mutilating her mother's splendid potatoes. Changeless Gordy, comfortable in his big striped coveralls. No. No. No. She couldn't blame him.

Night and nightmare jerk into wide awake, wide awake crying with resentment; Thursday night, all night, her father and Gordon in and outing, up with a sow, difficult in farrowing. Noises and night slip into wisps of dreams where a fat pink face comes closer and closer and her body swollen and stumbling cannot move away.

In the night you can be annihilated by despair. Then it's morning, and daylight makes the fears of the night seem like indulgences of self-pity. It's morning. A May morning.

She was up early, in the kitchen ahead of her mother. She cleared away the beer bottles, emptied the ashtrays, and washed the men's night off the table. She wanted to retch. Imagination. Too soon for morning sickness. The '59 mud-caked truck was parked outside the kitchen window.

"You were reading too long last night," Dinah said, and being her mother looked away to take the prying out of the words. "You're looking pale, darling. No exam's worth it. You'll do well anyway!"

At the hint of sympathy tears almost came but she swallowed hard to get the self-pity out of her throat.

"I just can't sleep. Perhaps I should go out and ride till I'm tired, but—such awful weather."

Her mother laughed, chuckled. "Wouldn't be love, would it? Dear Damion! Fatal for a girl to fall in love at exam time!"

"Oh Mum," she fenced and wished it were as gay and simple as her mother made it sound, her mother, skirting lightly on the edges of everything with a tolerant, passionless acceptance. She watched her spreading the bacon in a large orange skillet, her mother, combed, immaculate even to lipstick, always immaculate, even at seven-thirty in the morning. Why couldn't

24

she tell her? She didn't have to be sorry for her mother, didn't need to protect her. But Angela kept her panic to herself and threw a light answer back as deftly as Dinah had tossed a light question. "Well, Damion is kind of special, don't you think?"

"You bet he is," Dinah agreed and moved the bacon over with a rubber spatula.

Angela sat at the yellow table. Round the edges of the battered black truck the morning sky came in pink, the snow all gone. There's a fall of cigarette ash left on the window ledge by her father's place. Other girls could fight their mothers, throw failures at them to get back, punish them for petty ignorances and suspicions that had soiled small dreams. Why didn't she tell her mother now, her mother who'd cradled her in this silken cocoon of sweet reason. Why couldn't she tell her mother now, in the bacon-crisp morning kitchen, with her mother alone, and sunrise pink outside, and the scent of hyacinths creeping in from the other room like the scent of English woodlands skirting the streets of her mother's childhood. Why couldn't she tell her mother now?

"Mum."

"Oh damn. I've broken your egg."

"Mum."

"Will you get another mug down, darling. I'll sit and have a coffee with you."

My mother's eyes are not like mine. Hers are transparent. Mine opaque. She has fine hands.

"Mum."

She's sweeping the cigarette ash off the window-ledge into a white tissue, removing the traces of my father.

"What were you going to say, Angela? It kills me when both your father and Gordon are here smoking their heads off."

Gordon.

The chance has passed. The mood isn't right any more. Imagine the look of vague disbelief at the thought of Gordon . . . like her look for cigarette ash. Anyhow she holds a doldrum, a no-man's-land between herself and involvement, a wall. Has she ever cried? She didn't cry at Rory's funeral when even the neighbours cried—and I cried in the end. Does anything happen to my mother?

25

"Oh nothing. I was only wondering what to wear to the dance tomorrow. I was thinking Claire would like her wedding dance to be sort of pretty."

"Poor Claire." Dinah watched the rim of the sky past the truck over the rim of her coffee. "I thought that once she started teaching she would have broken with . . . Pity she came back to the district."

"She had a loan. She had to come back here for two years. Anyhow there was no choice of jobs last year."

"It was so nice to see her free, with a car and pretty things— after all the struggles."

Silence except for the coffee percolating again.

Angela watched the road past the truck. "Here comes the van."

She took up the pile of her schoolbooks. " 'Bye Mum, seeya." She ran past the truck without looking, then thumped as heavily as she could down the roadway that smelled of damp spring between the budding trees. The morning wind was already warm blowing at her hair. Damion would be looking out of the van window. If she runs hard enough and bangs her heels down hard, perhaps she can dislodge the thing inside her. The morning is suddenly spring, like being a child again. She jumps and leaps over the long puddles. Morning that takes away trouble. May morning. She wants to shout into the wind. This morning there's a hint of green across the poplar boughs, first green after winter catching at her consciousness so she can push worry on another track, side-track it, see it from afar. She remembers the same feeling at Rory's graveside. There was life in the warm chinook wind that afternoon. She had stood with mud on her shoes on the unctuous synthetic green of the funeral parlour grass and she had seen the wind teasing at the dry yellow stalks of prairie weeds beyond the feet of the mourners. She had been outraged by the self that could be distracted from its proper grief. But she had smelled the damp autumn earth and hated the properly composed faces of the neighbours dropping their tears for her brother. He was reaching the age when they wouldn't have liked him anyhow. Then when grief did focus on itself, its sharpness was indecently short-lived. She had blurred it in the maleness of a shoulder and the warmth of flesh against her lips, and had written a passionate assignment—to atone—all about the inevitability of man's neglect of his sorrows. "Delights like yellow butterflies flirting in the wind make man unfaithful to his sorrow."

New green tipping the poplars and a whiff of pine in her prairie roadway; she leaped over the puddle in the dip where the road meets the gateway. She twirled in the wind, her hair and coat flying. It's not real. She can't be pregnant on a new spring morning and a date with Damion tomorrow. She was flushed and laughing when she joined him on the school bus and her high held for the day. It was Friday; tomorrow she had a date. A date. A date.

All day she was above herself. She watched herself and it wasn't the way she wanted to be. She wanted to be cool like her mother, but, tired Friday and the girl showoff popped out, a force outside herself out of control. She watched Mr. Olson watching her and knew he missed nothing. She saw him assessing the thing between herself and Damion. Perhaps he was thinking that she was thinking she could trap Damion into . . . More suitable! Bridling under the scrutiny she flashed super clever-clever answers to hide herself behind.

It was Friday for Mr. Olson too; teachers' Friday. He felt the tired hostility. Minds had slipped away into the weekend's sociabilities, far from the rarefied decency of literature. He had lost his poets. On Friday he had lost the battle. They are wondering who is going with who, and what they will wear, and who will get the booze, will they get the car, and who pays the gas. On Monday they will be getting over it all, dull eyed and laughing coarsely. But Tuesday, Wednesday, and Thursday are his, to open cage doors, sometimes let a rare bird out.

He set them to write and sat watching. Let them write their hostility out on themselves, work it out.

Angela writes that *Death of a Salesman* transcends metaphor, is reality in absolute focus, experience shared raw. She writes and her mind is arguing on another track. He is certain I should get an abortion. He doesn't know what we're really like. We're good people. Crucifixion we toy with. After all, that was good enough for Jesus. But infanticide! Dear little bloodclot of a baby, cuty by-bies. Us-ums wouldn't hurt-ums, would-ums?

27

Mr. Olson, dear baby innocent Mr. Olson, you don't know nothing. Slay me but not motherhood. Nothing is private here. Maybe I could get it done in England. The magazines say it is easy in England. Nobody need know then. When I get off the plane, I could find a clinic in London, before I go to my grandparents'.

Mind on one track, fingers on another, writing words that say that once you have known Willie Loman you see him in the men of your community. She can't resist a Friday afternoon clever-clever to end on—"Literature makes us critics of our own society, therefore it behooves the sensible community to rid itself of the subversive activities of all literature teachers." Olé!

It was Joe Moynahan who was watching with his face to the window, watching the car turn round in the circle of the yard light, "Well, here he comes, young Good, in his father's Chrysler. Who the hell does he think he's taking out, the Queen of bloody Sheba?"

"Wow!" Damion said as he came in. "Wow! It's like walking into a Gauguin." Then he laughed as though he'd said something out of place. "You know, the artist," and he half pointed from the wide wooden bowl of polished red apples on the yellow table to the deep hazy blue of the wall round the uncurtained window, and over to the strident tapestry of red horses on a pink pasture hanging on the wall by the television.

Dinah opened her eyes wide and laughed delightedly. "Wow to you! That's the first time in nineteen years I've heard any-body—well—say a thing like that. Ah, I am no longer a stranger. Wow!" and she laughed again.

Joe grunted down into his plush chair and busied himself rolling a cigarette. "Don't keep my daughter out all night," was all he said, without looking up.

"Note," Damion joked as they walked round the dark Chrysler, "I cleaned the car, inside and out."

She didn't know what to say. She had washed her hair only an hour ago, shadowed her eyes, sprayed herself all over with the cologne her mother bought her from the Avon lady, per-fumed "To a Wild Rose". She had been ready and waiting—now she had nothing to say.

He smelled nice too, and the car interior new, leathery.

They both laughed·because they were both quiet as the gravel rattled under the wheels and they watched the headlights green-ing the new grass sprouting for spring by the road's edges. Beyond the headlights the flat miles spread black, only a few spaced twinkles of farm lights.

He was dressed up too; camel-coloured soft bell-bottoms, and his shoes polished. Funny to drive in silence. Peaceful. How long her legs are in pale stockings. "Do you want the radio on, Angela?"

"No. It's peaceful." She stretched her legs farther down. "Just drive on, drive on—into the black of the night."

So she wants to play it crazy. "Only as far, ma'am, as that star crashed on yonder horizon."

"That's a nice idea; prairie light a fallen star."

No follow-up. What do you say?

"I suppose you have done your homework?"

"Yes."

Mile by gravel mile the light spangles slipped from the horizon into the windows and door-light of Beupeur Hall. Its field was already almost filled with trucks and cars when the Chrysler turned in. The ground was mud underfoot and dark outside the glow from the windows of the hall. The building throbbed to the thud of feet stamping, and music beat out sobbing with a fiddle.

"Square dancing already; sounds like being a lively one tonight." He pushed her in front of him into the little plank porchway. Her hair shone white under the bare bulb and he caught its fragrance. They scuffed the mud from their feet on the muddied floorboards.

"Well, well, look who's here," cowboys with beer bottles tipped back in their hands welcomed them as Damion steered her through the crush into the stag line just inside the hall. There they waited, till the square dance ended, to take off their coats.

"My Dad built this hall when he first came to Canada," Angela volunteered, and looked again at the tall log hall, arched like a church, with tall windows and a thick, strong balcony where now a middle-aged orchestra was fiddling and throbbing out the music.

"I know. My Dad remembers when your Dad played the fiddle for dances, up there," he nodded up at the music.

"Funny," she said and tried to imagine it.

They had to reach over the older women who sat on benches along the sides to hang their coats on the six-inch nails that served as hangers, nails driven deep into the thick wood of the walls. When she raised her arms Angela felt the eyes outraged on her legs in their pale blue panty-hose. But she looked down and smiled into the faces, smiled down at the proper expressions under the stiff-sprayed hair, and she looked naughtily down right into the crease between Mrs. Farqua's bulging breasts, soft and old, almost out of the low-necked dress. "Hello, Mrs. Kopec," she said, being sunny to Gordy's dumpy mother, faded and fat-thighed, sitting there in a colourless stuffed sack of a dress with her legs too wide. Just about everybody was there.

Damion's arm was around her, steering her to where a young group confirmed for each other welcome and belonging. Not her group when she came with Gordon. Suddenly she was shy here, like the new girl, aware of glances, glad when the music cosied into a sentimental waltz. But it was hard to fit her feet to a strange partner. She had never danced with Damion before.

"Sorry," she said. "Sorry," again. Then she had the measure of him and his hand was powerful, a force high on her back making it easy.

"Funny to think of my Dad playing the fiddle up there," she made talk.

"He's said to have been a real jigging Irishman in his day."

She just laughed because it seemed sad.

"But this is a pretty super building to find in the middle of nowhere," Damion said, so they looked together up into the high beams and the good heavy wood.

"Funny to think of my Dad designing it. Perhaps that's what my Mum saw in him."

"They say he just swept her off her feet," he laughed and swung her off hers to end the dance.

"He-man, eh?" she said and loved it.

After the lunch when the crowd was thick and paper cups and serviettes littered the edges, Gordon came in and stood in the stag line. She saw him across her arm over Damion's shoulder, while they were in the crush close together, just swaying in the atmosphere, not talking. But her gaze got caught up in Gordon's bloodshot stare. She tried to look away but he had already pushed through to them, cut into their dance. Damion shrugged and let her go. Damn Gordon Kopec. He's taken her out for ages so he must have something. But damn, damn Gordon Kopec.

"Hi Gordy. You're pretty smashed, aren't ya?"

"Hi Ange," he pulled her close into his breath of stale beer and cigarettes, into the bearhug of his blue windbreaker, not dancing. She pushed him so he stumbled into some movement. Between the bobbing heads she saw Damion, partners away, dancing with the bride, the white veil swirling high.

Gordon was hard to hold off. The zipper in his jacket dug into her chest through her thin dress as he pulled her in tighter, breathing hot over her hair, in her face. She had her hands on his shoulders and tried to push him away. He just imprisoned her tighter with one arm on her back and freed the other to come between them and spread his hand hot, hard on her breast.

"For Christ's sake, Gordon, quit," she struggled against him. "Gordon, you're drunk." The dance surged hot in her face. He pulled her against his thigh and undulated against her in the crush of the people. Fury and humiliation choked her. She contemplated raising her knee and felling him when a man she didn't know, a man in a black Stetson, cut in and, giving Gordon a push, danced her off smoothly.

"Rough customer, miss?"

"Thanks," she said and felt pale, trembling, silly, not knowing where to look. But people would understand, be sorry for poor Gordy, losing his girl. She hoped Damion hadn't seen. It was all spoiled now, anyhow. She wanted to get away.

She excused herself, said she had to go to the bathroom, and made sure Gordon didn't see her go out.

After the hot hall, night was a fresh breath outside.

She walked slowly past the edge of the hall lights, into the cool and private dark across to where the two outhouses rose tall against the flat starred skyline. A light showed under the door of the women's privy, so she walked round the back and waited, voices whispering out into the night, intimate through the boards of the toilet.

A rising wind brushed through the dry stalks of last year's grasses. Angela shivered and hugged her arms round herself.

One of the voices raised itself, jerked out, "I'm telling you, I shall go mad if I'm like that again. I've told him it's time he started having his own bloody babies."

Then a low voice; she couldn't catch the words. A murmur.

"Oh no, he don't believe in the pill nor nothing like that. Says he'd kill me!"

The murmur again.

"Nutmeg in gin. Brought it on for you, did it?"

Angela trembled in the dark, squeezing her fingers hard into her crossed arms. Suddenly the smell of toilet disinfectant overwhelmed the spring night. She strained to hear.

"Grated nutmeg? Yes. In straight gin. As much as I can get in me on an empty stomach."

A long murmur.

"Well, I sure hope it works for me. I don't want to go through all that again."

Angela stood back and watched the heavy silhouettes of the two women follow the waver of a flashlight trail back to the lights of the dance. She opened the door to the privy and the stench of chemical toilet and new faeces got her. She ran and retched and threw up at the back of the hut. Had no tissue. Wiped her mouth on the back of her hand. Looked in the dark for a bit of blown paper to wipe off her shoes. She didn't want to go back in, but how long could she stand outside? When a group of women started out with a flashlight she crossed the mud and the porch and the stag line, was back where the dance was swinging wild and young, the old orchestra beating out all it had. She worked her way round the edge of the dancers and sat by the pot-bellied hot stove where the Indians were sitting, sat next to a young woman with braids whose enormous pregnancy unevened her skirt to lift it and expose the brown skin of her soft inner thighs. The Indian kids looked at blonde Angela curiously and she smiled for them, laughing harshly at herself inside, at the mind that would not stay on its misery. How beautiful and secret their dark eyes are. How beautiful.

She watched the dancers. Damion was dancing with the bride again, Claire, last daughter of a poor farm family, the first to go to university. Her bridal gown was simple, its back prolonged into a graceful suggestion of a train. She was flushed, talking with Damion as they touched and spun. How clever his feet were. The floor was muddy now. Mud on the dancing cowboy boots. Mud on the blue jeans. Mud on the trodden edges of the white gown, mud and torn places. The heel of a muddy boot caught the white stuff and the bride went on dancing as the hemline tattered and trailed muddied round her stained slippers.

It was hot and sleepy by the stove. One of the old Indian

women was wearing new mukluks, thickening the warmth with pungent smoked leather.

Damion came over and a little Indian girl moved so he could sit down.

A fight started in the stag line and somebody threw a bottle.

Mrs. Kopec was working her way round the hall with a dark brown instant coffee jar taking up the collection for the newly-weds. Angela went over to feel under the pile of the coats in her pocket for the dollar bill she had brought. She felt in both pockets. It wasn't there.

She wished she had brought some perfume. She felt she had a whiff of vomit about her.

"Let's go after this dance," Damion said. "It's getting ugly." He held her close and she smiled at him.

"You've got mad eyes," he said and spun her round swiftly.

"You've got Indian eyes—velvet."

"Your turquoise dress makes yours white—ice."

"Your brown shirt makes yours brown—molasses, muddy, moleskin—warm."

"White, fierce, agate—hot ice."

"Brown pools—cool."

"Opposites are good—they say. Let's go."

Gordon watched them go with a beer bottle tipped in his hand and his blurred water-colour eyes running red.

She was shy again. As Damion manoeuvred the long car out of the crowded field the headlights lit up necking and embraces. He laughed and leaned on the car horn to make an uproar, waved when anybody stopped what they were doing to look up.

"Highlights in the love life of our small world," he laughed and turned sharply onto the road home.

"Poor Claire," she said and wished she hadn't. She took off her shoes and put her feet up on the seat by the door, pretence of an ease she didn't feel with him.

"Yep. Poor Claire," he said and watched the road.

"Do you think she should have married him?"

"Hell, no."

There was a long pause. They both watched the road, then he leaned over and put the radio on loud, turned it down, then switched it off.

"Do you think she should have had an abortion?" she asked quickly, expressionlessly, keeping her eyes on the road.

"Not my business. I don't know." He was noncommittal but drove faster, then added like a joke, "But now they're married they're bound to live happily ever after." He reached his arm over across her shoulders and pulled her nearer, then held her hand on the seat between his soft camel pants and her pale blue nylon thigh, for silent miles across the dark prairie, the car like a lone ship isolated from the night.

"At least my Dad's not waiting up," she broke the silence as they turned, drove up the Moynahan roadway and the house lights were out.

"Are you coming out with me next week, Angie?"

"If I'm invited."

She felt his fingers live over hers and caught her breath.

"Christ, girl, you hold my hand and make me horny."

"Oh." She felt her face flush. Do guys really say things like that? Never Gordy. "Am I supposed to say I'm sorry?" She said it clever-clever, brittle.

He laughed and squeezed her fingers, brute, to joke. "You're supposed to be nice and lean against me and say, 'Me too.' Don't you know nothing, eh?"

"Not much," she admitted, sincere, then saved face saying, "except that you're a smoothy," then in a moment of candour that surprised herself, "You make me shy, Damion Good."

"Me too," he said as they stood by the kitchen door, leaned into each other, rocked gently together.

"Are you coming in?"

"No. Have to make an early start tomorrow. We're seeding. Got a lot to get in this year. Wow, woman," he said.

"Me too," she whispered, put her cheek against his, then slipped inside.

She stood in the dark room to watch his car lights turn out of the driveway and cut a shaft across the flat night.

She put her lips onto the back of her hand, bit into the flesh and let the tears run down. "Please God," she prayed. "Please God, help."

Rory had made the spice rack. Last night she had emptied most of the nutmeg from the little jar into an envelope and pushed it ready down in her jeans pocket. This morning she tiptoed through the house on bare feet, her jeans jacket over the flat half-bottle of gin she had found behind the wine glasses at the back of the kitchen cupboard.

She put the note she had ready on the table against the apples, picked up an apple then put it back, remembering "on an empty stomach". "Gone for a long ride," the note read. "Don't worry. Love, Angela."

She carried her boots and closed the door softly on the warm house still sleeping with hyacinths and apples. It was cold. She shivered as she pushed her feet into her boots and saw the morning, birds on bare branches, flitting, whimpering, crying; morning, flat and forever to the red beginning of the day. No leaves.

She had to get oats from the pig barn to catch her horse, stood by the barbed wire shaking the zinc bucket into the grey of the half-born morning. "Ami, Ami, Ami," she called and two horses came whinnying. Sometimes she let Rory's horse trail along, but—not today.

The two horses had been bought together when Rory was ten and she was twelve. That had been the last really good summer with Angela and Rory and their father with lots to do together, walking and grooming and teaching the geldings good manners. She fondled Rory's horse now, put her cheek against his and tricked him into staying behind the fence while she let Ami out. He whinnied and cried after them, rearing and pounding.

The bridles hung just inside the pig barn and as she reached for hers she saw a bottle of rye, half full, on the shelf among the veterinary things. She bridled her horse, left him with his lines hanging while she made her potion.

She funnelled the nutmeg down into the gin, shook it up, then, using the envelope as a funnel, filled the gin bottle up to its rim from the rye on the shelf. She took a deep breath and drank as much down as she could without breathing. But the nutmeg stuck in dry bits in her throat, her mouth. She had to breathe. She gagged on the spice and the liquor was like fire in her eyes. But the stuff had to go down. She held her nose like she'd learned to do when once she was sick and had had to take medicine. She held onto her nose and guzzled the rest of the stuff down her throat; fire and burning, scalding and razors in her eyes, gagging and gasping, leaning against the pig pen, not daring to let go the nose, with the pigs getting up to watch, sows grunting and piglets screaming. She had to get out before the racket brought her father to find out what was happening. She took a good swig from the rye bottle to swill her mouth and swallowed the fire; then one more gulp for luck, with deep breaths through the mouth to keep the stuff down. But the stench of the pigs was coming in through her mouth. She had to get out.

She wiped the neck of the rye bottle clean, very carefully, with a tissue from the big wad in her pocket, then she set the bottle on its side back on the shelf with its cap loose and the liquor trickling. The gin bottle she rammed in her pocket for disposal far away. Leave no traces. Switch the light off. Close the barn door—and away. It was done. It was started.

She rode bareback, urgently, her legs flailing from the knees like desperation at the horses's bay sides, urgent down her own grey roadway between the bare winter trees, turned north at the gate, kept up the gallop till she turned east at the road allowance onto the mud track where nobody would dare take a vehicle. Then she lay on the horse's rough neck and he slowed to a canter. She lay heavily letting his motion jolt through her body, letting his hard spine chop into her like pain blunted. The gin bottle bulged hurt in her pocket so she sat up, swung the bottle round in her hand, round her head, round and round, and she yelled like a film-Indian's bloodcurdle, let the bottle fly—out and away and to anywhere.

Ride. Ride. Ride. Ride. Ride for the lake where her brother

drowned, where there are hiding hollows in the land's undulations and rough empty miles of grey water, grey sage, grey sky with blood at the edges.

Sun shafted through. The horse was sweating, wet through her jeans, between her thighs, all down her legs. She was crying. Why? She never told herself to cry. She was cold. Jog and pound, jog and pound. Breasts tingling, tearing from the body; jog and tear, and jog and tear. She could hear herself crying into the sun-shafted morning, "I will not marry him, I will not marry him, I will not marry. Please God, please God, please God, let it be summer. Let it come right. Make it come right."

She jumped up and down on the pounding backbone of the sweating horse, jolting her back, bangety, BANG-BANGETY, bangety BANG BANG BANG BANG.

You can't throw up. Angela, you mustn't throw up. Got to keep the stuff down on an empty stomach, on an empty stomach. Behave yourself, Angela.

She took deep breaths through her mouth, then held her nose, and holding her nose began to laugh. She could hear herself laughing. Laughing, holding her nose, laughing, gasping down air, rocking back and forth, back and forth, and the horse only walking, walking. I'm drunk. I know I'm drunk. The road is wavy with mountains, up and down mountain road on a prairie. I'm Lady Godiva holding her nose. Keep the reins high Lady Godiva. I shouldn't have braided my hair; it should hang all around to hide my shame. What a shame. What a silly shame. This one little life, Angela. Yes sir. Stop being a silly female Angela. Pull yourself together.

She let go her nose and sat up tall. Just, quite simply, get an abortion Angela. Just a little blood clot Angela. Nutmeg and gin then he can have his own bloody babies. Fly bird. Fly.

She flopped forward and put her arms round the horse's neck, her face into the rough mane. Ami, Ami, Ami, help me, help me, help me. Fly Ami. Fly up and down the staggering mountain road, up and down Ami. Dance Ami dance. Let's be a circus. Ami my behind hurts. Let me lie on you, lie like a sack, a no-good sack. Thump into my belly. Thump thump thump. Angela don't let go the reins. Ami if I lose the reins don't you fall over them. Be a clever circus. Be a boat. Rocking swimming. Rocking in a swingboat. Fly bird fly. Rocking rocking. Ferris wheel fall-ing. I'm going to be sick. No. NO. NO. She contorted herself upright and took in breathing gulps through her mouth, held her nose again swaying round and round and round on her haunches. How long had she been riding? The sun was hot now and the sweat drying on the horse. The lake lay ahead. Lake in the prairie rocking, rock me on the waves of a prairie lake, rock me, rock me.

"Ami run. Go GO GO!" she yelled and struck him with her arms and legs flailing. "GO AMI GO!" She leaned into her knees and squeezed him faster, faster. She lay on his neck cry-ing, "Save me Ami, save me Ami, save me, go go go GO GO GO."

The sun was high when the pain seared and jerked her onto her knees, with the pebbles in the thin grass cutting. "Oh Ami help help me." She clutched at her belly. Pebbles rocking water over sky. White edge of water coming going insides retching. She gasped against the pains to undo her jeans and put her hands inside on the cold flesh of her quaking belly. Hard white crust by the edge of the water, water thundering. Pain. PAIN. "Please God," she moaned, "please God dear God make it happen." She retched the brown nutmeg slime out of her empty insides, knelt over the white edge of the water, retched and spit and retched and spit onto the clean pebbles under the white slime edge of the water. And the world turned round and round and I hurt. I hurt. An ache with a dagger in it. Abscess in a bruise bursting. Stand up now. Take a deep breath. Shake your head and stop the crazy Ferris wheel slipping. The belly is a wound. Warm hands hold it together; a wound in the sway of the world. I fell off my horse. I fell off. That is ridiculous. Ridiculous. "Ami where are you? Ami Ami Ami Ami."

She stood up dizzied to look around. No horse. Far down the lake, the lake still rocking. Her ribs hurt and her hip. She moved her hand around, felt it, pulled her jeans down to look. She must have landed hard on her hip. Giant bruise. And her face. She picked dried blood off it, off her temple, down by her eye and cheek, with the new sprouting grass green on the yellow rocking towards her. Holding her belly together with her hands still on her bare flesh she staggered to a hollow and lay face down with her hands cupped over her belly with the land turning over and over while water lapped and lapped over the sunheat and she was a boat rocking, rocking. She breathed deep and deeper to the lap of the hushing water and the lake was a sea in her ears, rocking, rocking, cradle rocking.

A breeze scratched through the dead sage. The earth was cold underneath her and the sun hot on her back. The lake lay still with a speckled duck and three ducklings. New green shoots all in the yellow around her. Today it is summer. There will be leaves on the trees when I get home. Am I going home? She separated a tissue from the wad in her pocket and pushed it down inside her jeans, looked at it. Nothing. It hadn't happened. Oh God, it hadn't happened. And I am a bruise.

She walked unreal along the alkaline rim of the water, aching, found a deep place that was almost a pool, took her boots off, rolled up her jeans, crouched knee-deep, sluiced her face and the edges of her hair and her open mouth, and saw diamonds dazzle in the ragged little waves, saw—forgetting.

Gulls swooped. Ducks rode the waves. Coots and sandpipers paddled and ran in the water—and the rings they start in the water reach outward and outward like rings of pain. And I am watching the birds, not concentrating properly on the proper pain. Madness is only at the middle, the edges are sane rings touching diamonds, ripples, rings of sorrow flowing outward to diamonds on ripples. Your one little life, Angela. It's summer. There will be leaves on the trees at home.

She pulled her boots on, found the soggy envelope in her pocket, brown-stained from the morning. She shredded it and dropped it in fragments, bit by bit, like dirty snowflakes to float and bob in the alkaline edge of the wind-shaggy waves.

She stood in the sun, undid her braids, shook her hair free, walked away from the lake calling her horse, dragging her jacket along on one finger. The heat beat down, poultice on an abscess, wound on a bruise, summer through a thin shirt.

I can't walk in a straight line. I am lurching. I can't do anything more. Please God, I tried. God I hurt; I can't do anything more. "Ami Ami," she kept calling through the haze of her emptiness and step by careful step crept through the daze to where the horse was grazing new shoots, heading home. She took his lines and leaned against him, hurting. She put her arm across to jump herself up, then gave up. I hurt Ami. Let's walk.

So she walked him home to where nothing had changed.

"Are you hurt bad, my lovely?" her father asked, holding her and looking her over, the father of his little girl again. "Go on now, I'll see after Ami. You go in to your mother."

"No, there's nothing you can do, Mum. Just let me sleep."

And she slept for all the missed hours of a week of nights, while outside the trees slipped into leaf, while . . . nothing had happened.

At last. Relief. It was all behind her. As the plane settled into flight across the prairies it was as though she came into sharp focus again out of the two-month haze of her fear and unreality. Sanity, sharp and exhilarating, came to the centre again; panic retreated, a distant ripple, to the edges of her being. She was flying. Away. She need never come back now she had got away. Maybe she was never coming back—ever, so now she looked down at the pattern of the prairie with a first-time-last-time perceptive affection. A land cut up in such tidy packages that its own rivers, jagging and twisting as they did across the level-edged divisions of gold, looked like primeval irrelavances to man's well-ordered intentions. Now a lake with an alkaline border. Now a dried-out alkaline bed. Smudges in the sunshine—mistakes, the slaked-out bone of pre-prehistory. And she was flying away. Reprieved.

Grandmother Dawson had poured out such long letters of encouragement and welcome as the time for Angela to travel had grown closer. She had written with an excitement as though having Angela staying would be like getting her daughter back. "Isn't life funny," she had written, then repeated herself the next time and the next time. "Your mother was just your age when she left us." The repetitions hadn't mattered. Angela had grown to hope for those blue airletters in the mailbox when she got off the school van. A moment to catch a love-look from Damion, then an airletter in the mailbox from the grandmother she had never seen, but who was there, a sanctuary on the other side of the Atlantic.

Because she was sure she was going away she had been able to see leaving as an end to her problems. She had just had to get through the last month—and the sickness. Most mornings in June she had had to take deep breaths to keep hold on her nausea. Twice it hadn't worked and she had had to leave class and lock herself in a toilet, trying to vomit quietly lest anybody

42

came in and heard. It had been difficult to write the early morning exams, checking off the endless pages of squares in little boxes on answer sheets for machine scoring. Maybe nausea would have blurred her vision, made her put check marks in the wrong row of squares. Then Damion will get the scholarship. She looked out into the clouds as the plane went higher, a solid floor of clouds. It's deceptive. You might think you could walk on the clouds.

Damion would be on the tractor now, summerfallowing with his shirt off under the shade of the tractor's orange umbrella. Without even closing her eyes she could remember the scent of sage grass stiff in her hair; the stars were not in the sky, my love, they are still bursting bright here in my head, above the clouds in a jet plane.

"Great if we feel the same, next year, when we both get back," he had said and thrown a pebble from the thin grass by his hand into the moon on the water.

Plane engines in and out of her listening while she remembers summer night heat and lake water lapping, and him lying squinting at the sky with one hand touching hers, she saying nothing, not daring to know about next year. "Perhaps you'll meet a beautiful Eskimo girl and never come south again," she had said at last and touched his leg with her bare foot.

"Not likely. Could be I'm hooked on a blonde. Anyhow I'm going up north for the big money; to come back with it."

"Greedy."

"Well, you'll probably come back all independent, militant liberationist."

She had sat up and watched the white edge of the water in the moonlight, pushed next year away as now she watched the pink-edged clouds, letting next year run on in dreams like a soppy television commercial, the two of them running to meet each other in camera-slowed motion with soft winds and choirs of music. If she got an abortion in London—maybe—if the feeling lasted—if she got an abortion maybe she could come back to Damion, to her horse and summer—and her parents. Can you go back to your parents? Her parents?

At the airport she had watched her Dad being so attentive to her, her Dad wearing his best suit, plying her with food and drinks in the coffee bar, listening to all the announcements with his head on one side, knowing for a few brief moments the role to play with the young woman who was his daughter. He was almost debonaire and it tore at her heart strings, the pathos of it, because they had so little to say to each other. She smiled at him and for a few minutes the Dad of her childhood paid court to her, that affectionate, kindly father she had lost once her own ideas had shaped and he had never tried to understand them. She wanted to love him. He muttered words of abuse as long-haired bearded travellers and girls wearing jeans and carrying backpacks came through the airport, but there were tears in his old eyes when she went up the ramp and left them.

"Have a fabulous time," was all her mother had said. She had been flushed and elegant, a woman to look at again.

It is like an algebra problem. When a plane is going east at 660 miles per hour and a farm truck is going in the opposite direction at 55 miles per hour, what is the distance between child and parent after the lapse of two and a half hours? The distance has not changed. It is still infinite. My father died when I was twelve and a half, the day I answered him back and knew he was not always right. My mother? If I met her at an airport I would like her, would ask, "Who is that interesting woman?" But it's only the look she has. Only an interesting stranger. Then why didn't I tell her, right at the beginning? Maybe I could have been flying now—carefree, totally. For sure she would have thought like Mr. Olson. In some way her mother and Mr. Olson were the same, except he knew more about you because you wrote so much of yourself for him over the years. And while her mother often retreated into vagueness he never missed a thing. Angela had watched him watching her those terrible mornings when she struggled to keep her nausea down and knew she had gone pale. She had resented his noticing. Why? She had avoided him too. Why? He would have helped her. He had stopped her in the corridor one afternoon, at the change of classes when crowds were pushing both ways. He was on his way up from the staffroom; she could smell the touch of other people's cigarette smoke on him as he stopped her.

"Angela." It had been an effort. She didn't know whether he

was embarrassed or reticent. "Is there anything I can do to help you?" He noticed the skin tight on her jaw and the shadowing of her eyes that wasn't put on, thought he saw the barest message like pain cross those opaque eyes.

"No. I'm all right. I can cope," she said, instead of clinging to his offer. She heard herself sound brusque, rude. Why?

All he said was, "You know best," and he touched her shoulder sympathetically so she had to thrust her chin up to ward off tears.

But that was all over now. Mr. Olson I am flying over another world of other people. Nobody knows me down there. Now there were forests far below and lakes. She stretched happily lifting her arms and sighing out loud. The woman next to her looked back from the paperwork she had been at ever since they'd become airborne, the little table covered. She smiled and leaned over to look out the window.

"Great, big, beautiful, wonderful world," she said and leaned back in her seat. "I love going places."

"It's my first time—anywhere," Angela volunteered and laughed after saying it. It sounded so naïve.

The woman laughed. "I was over forty before I took flight, so to speak." She stretched back luxuriously, her eyes deep in crow's-feet and grey strands in the coarse black of her hair.

Angela looked at the papers on the table.

"I'm on my way to a conference," the woman explained, "and typical of me, I'm finishing the paper I'm giving tomorrow, now. Lord how I procrastinate! The story of my life!"

Angela surveyed the open briefcase on the floor stuffed with magazines and paper-cuttings. "What are you talking about?" she asked, smooth like a casual traveller.

"Oh, theatre for children," the woman smiled, calm, mature, and wondered at the frown crossing the brow of the girl who had turned to assess her. What unusual eyes, and an intensity that is collecting me like a beachcomber finding a rare seashell, holding me to her ear. She smiled and spread her hands in help-less mockery of the extravagance of the worlds she could hear coming, "I'm a dream maker. You know, civilizations fade and perish but the dreams their children dreamed live on—must make dreams—"

Angela wrinkled her nose and did a sharp shrug. "Well, I almost went to the theatre, live theatre, once. Almost. Once. But it snowed. The vans wouldn't go out." She laughed again because it sounded so naïve.

"You'll make up for that while you're in Europe, they do a lot for their children; they like them. How long are you staying?"

"Supposedly for a year, a year before university. But maybe I'll just stay for ever. I have grandparents in England."

"Well, good luck! One of my daughters came for a year like that four years ago. Watch out, things grab you and before you know it you're all caught up in some wild project, living in some smidgin of a flat, all gone on the romance of a multi-coloured cosmopolitan back street. See, I see your eyes light up just at the words."

"Sounds nice."

"My daughter, at the moment she's an assistant stage manager for some godforsaken theatre group. Lives in an attic room at the top of a back-street united nations."

Angela looked wistfully at the earthy delight in the woman's lined face and she felt herself stirred by the enthusiasm of the voice. She sighed. Great, big, beautiful, wonderful world, she thought.

"What do you think you are going to do with your year?" The question was warm, a probing encouragement, the sort Mr. Olson gave, to romantic plans and big ideas.

But the answer came out flat, a sharp little chasm of despair plonked in the space between them. "I guess I'm going to have a baby, most of the time," and she turned to look down to the ice-patterned earth. Always winter. Grey or ice-blue. And a long silence. The woman was looking at her profile so she bent her head so that her hair fell forward, a curtain, this morning's shampoo scent against her senses, shampoo a continent ago in the blue bathroom.

"I'm sorry," was what the woman said, then she was silent. That's not what the women at home would say. No, it isn't nice.

Then Angela turned sharply to look straight at the woman who hadn't turned away. "I procrastinate too. I should have got an abortion." She watched for a recoil, a shocked response. Just

46

words. It wouldn't be that easy where I came from—but the words sound worldly. The woman neither recoiled nor looked away. She rubbed her nose and frowned slightly. "Surely it's not too late. You're slender as a morning shadow—and extremely beautiful," she added with a little chuckle that took the sentimentality away.

"Really? Thank you." Angela rubbed her nose now, and smiled shyly. "Nobody ever told me that before. Anyhow, it hasn't done me much good." She heard herself using this woman as a confessional. "I never even had a boy friend, a proper date, until the last few weeks."

"You could have got his photograph. Easier than carrying his baby with you!" Angela gasped inside and laughed out, shocked. What an outrageous thing for a nice motherly woman to say. Could she outrage her back and tell her the truth. No. The truth was too crude. Damion had made her familiar with the freedom of outrageous thoughts, but . . . she flushed now at the idea that Damion—the woman saw the flush, then the ghost of a frown cross the girl's face—Damion was not easily familiar. Me too, he said, laughed and turned away with an affectionate brush of the lips. With Damion there were no hostage moments to bind—except in her father's mind. "The sooner you get on that plane, away from that Loverboy Fancypants, the more to my liking. Not enough shame to pull the grass out of your hair. I've known his sort before!" Ugly. Ugly.

The woman watched trouble wash out the last of the laughter. "Life doesn't end because of a baby, you know, whatever you decide to do about it." She pulled a funny face and spread her hands again. "Damn it all, I had four accidents. Oh, I was married. But four times I thought I was finished, kaput, done for. But I got around to my life in the end. Late, but I'm still alive and loving!"

Angela put her feet up on the back of the seat in front and studied the golden hair on her long bare legs. "You sound like Women's Liberation," she said and laughed in case it was the wrong thing to say. It was either a joke or a condemnation in her experience.

"Oh loosely, I suppose," the woman answered slowly. "It's so hard to know at any given time if we are making the right

47

choices. All we can do is face up to the—confusion of . . ."

"Security is daring to admit the uncertainty at the centre of everything—quote from my teacher," Angela contributed.

"Right," the woman agreed swiftly. "Bang on! And all we can do is feel out the place we are in and try to be honest." She chuckled. "Oh I loved my accidents, but, somewhere at the edge of me there was always a discontent and longing for the me who had to step aside and wait."

"Divine discontent," Angela added and they smiled together. "My boy friend said it's the men who need liberating from their—insecurities."

"If he understands that, then all I can say is, he is a very naughty young man to be letting you go travelling with a bundle." That statement came out too sharply.

Angela crimsoned. "He doesn't know." And she blushed again inside the crimson. No. Damion wouldn't have. He wasn't ready to give hostages. She shut off from the woman's attack and watched the icy desolation below.

The woman went back to her papers, shut out. Periodically during the rest of the flight they drifted into odd forays of unimportant conversation, shared meals and drinks, the woman not prying and Angela playing it cool, adolescent nonchalance making her safely unapproachable. So what? She was flying, suddenly an instant world traveller. Competent. It took only once. Yesterday a jet plane was still a mystery, but today she was a traveller, walking casually to a washroom high above her continent. She had thought it might be difficult, that she might be a gauche farm-girl. But already it was ordinary. She was coping, adapting to the role. Even the woman in the next seat, so forthright, unlike any woman she had ever met except as a voice on C.B.C. radio, even she—just once, and the woman was her people.

Angela was coping in free orbit, flying high. She raised her chin and hardened her eyes—cool cat, cool cat.

The mood persisted as she followed the flow of world travellers through the rigmarole of customs, world traveller arrived in London.

She changed her first traveller's cheque. Not difficult. Then she sat on her luggage to examine the foreign notes and coins, excited all the while by the pathos of legs in a hurry dragging with baggage, the shouting of porters. Funny accents that made her mother's seem like pure American. She sat by the wall at the edge of the movement on her red flight bag bought especially for this journey, and she felt that at last she was at the heart of the world, herself, Angela Moynahan, right in the throb of London. She leaned against the wall smiling and tried to calculate backwards what would be happening now at home. About four in the morning. Birds calling to themselves in the whispering caraganas. Her parents in bed unaware of the red edge on the sky. Damion in bed.

Shouting, gesticulating porters pushed passengers and burdens of baggage into a flow of taxis. Angela watched to see the way it was done, looked through her coins to find one that seemed small enough to be given away as a tip, then she moved forward into the line of shouting action, dragging the brown case her mother had travelled with nineteen summers ago in one hand, her new red flight bag in the other, and the large, brilliant bag her mother had made to hold all the oddments of travel across her shoulder.

"Taxi, luv? Taxi!" and she was swept away through the mad streets of London to the hotel they had booked for one night through the travel agency. Dumped by the porter, confused in the foyer, but then—coping. Another small coin for the man who carried her bags into the elevator, the lift. Ancient man. Ancient lift. Ancient dignity. She watched fascinated, cool traveller, as he cranked it by hand, actually wound it and himself and her and her two bags up the shaft, creaking and clanking like a horror chamber all the way. Then she was closing the door in her own hotel room in London, England. Oh, the bigness of the first breath of a green-carpeted room with a greencounterpaned bed and the strange carpet-cleaner smell of a hotel room—the first hotel room ever. She went to the tall window and looked out, looked down into London. The back of the hotel, backs of other tall buildings, an ironmongery of fire-escapes, and at the bottom a junk yard of narrow streets and garbage cans and parked vehicles and in the middle of it all a walled-in schoolyard, grey, with boys in white shirts with bare knees, all of them chasing one other boy exactly the same; white shirt, bare knees, all the shirts sliced by a dark tie. Work-men standing around, some with shovels, like toys shovelling debris of a broken building onto a truck. Ugly lovely romance, the brute iron and concrete sad heart of man, Mr. Olson. So many things to make words for, Mr. Olson.

She pirouetted across the room and bounced up and down on the green raised flowers on the green counterpane. She switched the radio on and felt like a traveller because the voice coming out was foreign and the mood of the noise foreign, and she turned the dial from station to station, exploring—how funny. She was here!

Bathroom along the corridor to your left, the ancient dignity in a green uniform had told her. Along a green corridor through a cream door into a green bathroom with a white bath on gold lion legs. And up a step, two steps, to a white toilet—ah-ha, like a throne. Englishman on his throne dreaming of lions and seeing himself in a long mirror. She stood to take stock of herself, did a wild dance around on the worn green of the linoleum sea, lifting her arms and swinging the mane of her hair. Mirror, mirror on an English wall, she bent up close to her own reflection and teased her own white eyes—extremely beau-tiful, the woman said. But, my dear, she was old, never kid yourself, and Angela Moynahan laughed at herself. My dress is short but the English girls seen from the taxi window were wearing them two inches shorter. She sang along the sober English hotel corridor, brushed her hair in her own room, changed into the turquoise smock, a delicate thing with long sleeves, as short without pants as the English girls' dresses. This is liberation, to put all you need in the bag on your shoulder, put your own room key in last and jaunt off out like freedom on wings to take in the roar of London.

50

On her way out she peered in at the hotel dining-room, very formal with white tablecloths and old waiters. It looked as though it cost the earth to dine in there, besides plucking up the courage to go in. She went on out into the heat of the summer street with so many people to walk among, get lost among, a throng of walkers, and Angela Moynahan walking among them. Mr. Olson was right when he said even Calgary wasn't a city like the old cities of the old world.

The noise, the bustle, the excitement got into her, so she walked and walked, a flash of summer prairie in the city streets; her space-tanned long legs skipping among the more sedate ones of busy workers and tired shoppers weighted with shopping bags. The turquoise smock was vivid as the room it had been stitched in, fresh as the scent of hyacinths, and people smiled back at the girl who still had the glow of the open spaces on her. She kept skipping. She wanted to sing. Sometimes she forgot and ran because there were a few yards of open space ahead through the walkers. Then she'd feel silly and stop to gaze in at shop window displays, then walk away again almost sedately until she forgot and swung her shoulder bag with its stitchery of bright peacocks to the rhythm of her exultation. Sunshine in city streets, and city birds clamorous, insistent at the tops of buildings; red double-deckers and darting taxis; people of every colour and style; a woman passing with pink hair and nobody mocking. So many people together and alone, crowded and private. So many people seeing but not watching. In my prairie spaces people are watchers, like damp law, so when you feel your dreams on fire you hide away from people, you find a secret place and call out to the sky and dance your joy into the wind, a gift to the private earth. Sometimes you get a bit of it into an assignment for Mr. Olson, with a struggle to find the words. In this crowded street I can talk to myself. I think I could do cartwheels without causing a gossip. I feel like a red balloon bouncing along over the heads of the people, they look up and they smile and pat me up again; up and up bounding in the sunshine, on and on. How long have I been walking?

Suddenly she was tired. She turned up a quieter little street, greyer, less peopled, and stopped to study the crowded windows of a second-hand store, pictures and carved furniture and sets of fine china, a jumble of personal histories. She walked on past dingy warehouses and stopped again at a café that looked poor, a coffee bar and two tables, neither posh nor terrifying. It wouldn't be wildly expensive. She dared to go in.

She sat up at the counter and wondered what to order.

"Tea, luv?" the woman asked, coming at her with a big metal pot.

"No. Coffee please."

"You American, eh?"

"Oh no," Angela found herself answering emphatically. "I'm Canadian. From the wild wild west," she added, enjoying the sound of it in the sombre little café.

"You want it black, luv? Sam there," she nodded her head towards the end of the counter, "he's an American. That's right, isn't it Sam? One of me regulars. Eats here every day, he does, after the rush."

The bent back two stools away pulled itself up and turned round bringing a book in its hand as though loath to be interrupted. A red Afro with a red beard under it. Red Santa Claus with long eyes crinkling into a full smile. "Wow. Wow. Come in, sunshine. Sure. I came from the U.S.A. Never seen you here before."

"No. I just arrived. From Calgary to London."

"Hey. You know Banff then. I spent a winter in Banff— ski-bumming."

"Yes, I know Banff," Angela said doubtfully measuring his wildness and scratching at her memory to recall the mountains and the gift shops from the one afternoon she had been there, a family outing when she was ten or eleven.

"Small world," he said. "Should I join you?"

She wasn't sure but she smiled. God knows what trash, her father would say. Sam moved his meal and his book and sat himself on the next stool.

"Anything to eat, luv?" The waitress was hovering. Panic. What to order? She looked at the brown mess of beans on Sam's plate. "Beans like that," she pointed.

"I'm Sam Lubinkoff. From Montana. We're nearly neighbours —except that I've been away four, coming five, years."

He's younger than he looks, not so fierce as he looks. "Angela. Angela Moynahan, from southern Alberta."

"Small town?"

"No. Farm."

"Small world. Me too. Farm kid. That makes us like family in this big city eh, Angel?"

"I read that too," she said pointing to his book, *Night Flight*. "In fact we had this teacher who was crazy about Saint Exupéry," she went on talking for something to make conversation because he was terrifyingly alien to her. She found him formidable, a wild unknown. "This teacher used to quote from Guillaumet, you know, 'To be a man is . . .' "

" 'Precisely to be responsible'," he ended the quote with her. "Sure I know, Angel," he laughed out of the fire of his face and she laughed. Mr. Olson's quotation in a London café. Small world. Silly, crazy small world.

"Small world," he said. "A countryman of yours gave me this book. See what he put in front." She looked close at his face close to hers as he pushed the open flyleaf at her, red gull face with long eyes stretched backwards, fierce grey glints of ice seen from an airplane. Fierce face. She read the inscription at the top of the page, in the small spiky handwriting of one Bill Polonski of Ontario, "between travellers passing". The handwriting had gone on in level careful lines to copy out the words of airman Magee's "High Flight".

She laughed to find the familiar thing there and read aloud, " 'Oh, I have slipped the surly bonds of earth'," and felt that she meant it. "That comes out of our classrooms too," she told him. "There'll be snow falling forever and somebody will read, 'Sunward I've climbed and joined the tumbling mirth of sun-split clouds—' " She sighed. "This year it snowed when it should have been summer. Winter. Winter. More winter," she said and he saw summer in eyes like butterflies.

"This winter I felt 'cabin'd, cribb'd, confin'd, bound in'," she confessed, remembering snow at the windows.

" 'Like a falcon towering in her pride of place was by a mousing owl hawked at and killed'?" he quoted, teasing and like a question. She frowned. "Touché," she said. "Yes, I ache to soar. And all hail to you, Macbeth."

"Say, Angel, you and me could fly high together, should we?" he invited and brought her back to her uncertainty, to a hard stool, a drab café, and a wild and fearful stranger.

"I've never talked to anyone with so much—" she drew with her hands swirls of lines round her face, miming beard and hair "—so much hair," she said and she laughed because it sounded so naïve.

"Don't you be scared, luv. He's a bit of all right behind that thornbush," the waitress butted in and made them both laugh. "He's a nice guy, luv."

He cocked an eyebrow at the waitress and laughed. "Well, come to that, I've never talked to anybody with angel eyes. Not many people are given the right name."

"Idiot," she said. "What are you doing in London, anyway?"

They leaned together, suddenly easy, and laughed into each other's eyes, strangers meeting in free orbit, travelling. His eyes crinkled and hers opened wider as they talked.

"Some study, some work, mainly study—yet. I play the violin."

"You're kidding!"

"No. Really. You can come and help me tonight, if you like."

"Oh yea?"

"Yea. You can hold the hat—and look beautiful."

"You're joking."

"No, honest. I've got a busker's licence."

She looked at him blankly. "You're talking outside my vocabulary. What do you have a licence for?"

"Don't they teach you nothing in them little towns back home, honey child? You come with me tonight and I'll give you a lesson in the street ways of the great big world, eh? But that's tonight. There's a lot of afternoon left. I'll show you around if you like?"

"I like," she answered blithely and knew she shouldn't. She shouldn't be picking up with God knows what sort of trash, a stranger unshaven, therefore unclean, a threat.

She sorted through the strange money and he helped her work out the coins to pay for her meal while the waitress mocked accents with them.

"Make sure you take her to see Buckingham Palace," was the last thing she called after them as they stepped out into the street heat of cement and old bricks. He led her further into the back streets.

"I'm a slummer," he volunteered, "a connoisseur of back alleys and decay—London, Paris, Beirut, Lisbon, or Saigon, wherever you like. It's the back streets are the city for me, as much as the parks and the palaces."

They walked along the hot pavements talking, talking. He had travelled around for a couple of years after he got back from his tour of Vietnam. "I couldn't settle," he said. "Too much horror, murder, in my head." Eventually he had decided to settle in London and pick up his music again.

"You're not going home again—to Montana?"

"I didn't think so, but today, Angel, you've made me homesick. You've brought it all back, summer and big skies and the lakes."

She sucked her cheeks in and grunted. "But it isn't just a great landscape . . ." They remembered the inconveniences of isolation and the hates and the intolerances of the people with sunlined faces.

"Not hate," he said. "I've worked things out since I've been away from it all. It's fear. Fear of innocence, somehow."

Angela watched her sandalled feet walking on the hot flag-stones, and like a city kid she hopped to miss treading on the lines, and she calculated fear or hate? Fear or hate? If my father could see me walking down a warehouse back street with a long-haired stranger wearing an army tunic with a book in its pocket! He would hate this stranger. She walked backwards with long strides. "Are you innocent, Sam? Sam the American?" she asked into his eyes, then twirled around away from his answer.

"Only if you are, Angel," he said.

Then they wheeled and soared like crazy children through the crazy alleys calling highflight crazy to each other:

—" 'I've chased the shouting wind' "—
—" 'up, up the long delirious, burning blue' "—
—" 'topped the wind-swept heights' "—
—" 'where never lark' "—
—" 'nor even eagle' "—
—" 'flew' "—

Then they walked hand in hand in the proper places, finished the lines of "High Flight" together, " 'And, while with silent, lifting mind I've trod the high untrespassed sanctity of space, put out my hand, and touched the face of God.' "

"But only in space," she said and ran away quickly round the rim of the fountain outside Buckingham Palace. Then she sat on the stone edge to scrounge in her bag for two Canadian nickels to throw into the water.

"That's a fantastic design," he said, picking up her shoulder bag and holding it from him to examine both sides. "It's wild. Wild, man. Did you do it, Angel?"

She looked at it as he held it up. "It is a bright thing, isn't it. No, not me. My mother. I like it."

"Lordy. Must be some mother. It's her own design and everything?"

"Sure. Our house is full of creations. This is one of her small ones."

"You're kidding. Does she show them? This is fantastic."

"Honest?" She took the bag from him and smoothed it out across her knees and tried to see it as he was seeing it. "It's my mother's thing, I guess."

"She must be wild."

Angela shrugged and looked at him vaguely and tried to bring her mother into perspective. She pictured her sitting with her feet tucked under her, her head on one side, watching her fingers stitching; or rocking placidly at the old treadle machine. "No. My mother is a very cold woman. Non-involved."

"Not the woman who thinks like this," he traced his finger across the variations of texture on two peacocks as they lay across her knees.

Funny. I never thought of looking for thinks in a piece of sewing," she mused and frowned at the idea. "I had a boy friend who came into our kitchen and said it was like getting inside Gauguin." She laughed. "Would you believe I didn't know who Gauguin was. I looked it up in the encyclopedia in the school library. I still don't know really except in words. I'm telling you there is no pale paint in our house. It used to embarrass me when I was a kid."

"Well, if this were mine I'd hang it over my altar," he said, spreading his big hands over it.

"Okay. I'll leave you half of it in my will. How'll that be, eh?" She laughed and hooked the bright thing over her shoulder and they went off walking across to St. James Park, park in the middle of a city, with people and lovers and mothers and children and tramps and hippies and everybody on the green of the green grass. Angela stroked the grass. "I had a high school teacher who used to tell us about the touch of English lawns," she said. "Soft and cool."

"And green growing green."

"How big the trees are. You could live under the shade of one tree."

They lay on their backs on the edge of a puddle of shade looking through the green stretch of the branches to glimpses of pale English sky.

"Confession," she said. "I've never seen a tree as big as this. We have eighteen years of trees round the house at home—my mother has a craze for planting trees—but none as big as this. Poor prairie poplars. I used to sit right in the caraganas, make sort of—dens of green peace. You look like a red Santa Claus on a green page, Sam, Sam the American."

"So you're the Angel at the top of my green Christmas day."

"Hot sun in the cool shade of a London tree with the city passing so near. Who would ever believe it? A green bubble of quiet."

"Interlude."

She turned on her stomach and let her face rest on the cool grass. "Have you ever smelled bluebells, Sam the American?"

"Mmm, mmm," was all he said, the bearded stranger who felt like the feeling that home ought to be. His hands were behind his head and his eyes were squinted to think some thought beyond the edge of the branches. A noise of birds chirping and cheeing invaded the air. Foreign birds. Different sounds. Traffic roared on the edge of the green shade. The buildings of London pushed against the crowded sky. The city sun was hot on her back and the grass summer cool, to breathe in. She drifted off to sleep, tired traveller.

When she woke up she rolled onto her back and sat up. The red Santa Claus was still there. She looked up through the trembling height of the tree where he was looking and the roar of London traffic swept back into her.

"Hi," he said. "Welcome back."

"Sorry. I must have been tired. I have less than two days to get the feel of London—and I have to go to sleep." She shook her head.

"Time to go. Work looms," he said and gave her his hand to pull her up. She stood and brushed her hair from underneath, smoothing its pale length.

"You must have Swedish ancestors or Finnish," he said, watching her. "Is your father a tall blond Scandihoovian?"

"No. He's a middle-sized brownish Irishman with brown flecks in his eyes. I'm some sort of positive throwback. Your ancestors must have been Vikings?"

"Scottish, mainly. That's the red. I suspect a Negro somewhere for the curl. Say, you're going to need something warmer on if you're coming to hold the hat for me."

They walked along swinging their joined hands, talk, talk, talking. Somewhere in the middle of a sentence they jumped onto a double-decker, scrambled up the reeling stairway. "I've never done this before," she giggled and fell into the front seat at the top and laughed to see London so spread out and busy. Then they had to get up and off again, lurching along the swaying crazy length of the top deck, laughing and hanging on to get down the stairs, then daring to jump off onto the flying pavement before the wheels had stopped turning.

He waited in the antique prim foyer while she went up to her room to make herself warm enough for the first English evening. She put on pale panty-hose and shoes and got out the fringed shawl she had never used anywhere yet. Her mother had made it just in case there were any special occasions. A voluminous soft woollen thing, violent blue with a stitchery of fiery dragons curving and stretching along the edges. She draped it round her pale self, a deeper cocoon. She tilted the dressing-table mirror so she could see farther down herself, lifted her arms so the shawl spread like wings. She took the jar of creme sachet, a gift from the Avon Lady at home, out of the peacock bag, touched it here and there, and left the green hotel room, its carpet-cleaner staleness, with a lingering hint of To a Wild Rose.

Happiness is being here. Heaven is just being, not watching, anticipating or remembering, just being here. Happiness I am

58

here. And she went down in the cranked elevator as though she were drifting down a wide celestial staircase.

"Wow!" was all he said, and smiled.

Another run round the streets, another double-decker, a dash into his basement flat to change his shirt and pick up his violin and put on a cheeky English chequered cap.

"You're a long way from Montana," she said as they walked up the steps from his cellar yard talking back to the black children with their noses pushed through his palings watching them.

"I love it, all of it," he laughed and waved back at the kids and rushed Angela along to an entrance to the Underground. Escalators down down down, posters, writings on the wall, people, a rush, a kaleidoscope, then they were outside his theatre.

He put the cap in her hand, set his violin case on the cobblestones of the alley that ran alongside the old theatre, where the queue turned round from the front entrance and waited for the cheap seats. What was she to do? She felt silly standing there in the dingy narrow alley with the chequered cloth cap in her hand, a line of people looking through her and idly watching.

She moved from foot to foot, wrapped her shawl around her and looked up at the towers and walls closing her in, looked down again at Sam the American rubbing rosin on his bow. "Can you imagine what the P.T.A. ladies would say if they could see me now," she leaned to him and giggled, anything rather than look at the thin line of people along the wall. A lot of young people—which made it worse to be standing with the cap in her hand, on show. She put her shoulder bag on top of his violin case. "Inspiration," she said, to fill her silence. "Musician, strike your strange instrument." She looked from him raising his violin to the prairie peacock in an alley blazing and felt the show-off girl rising in her. Sam the American began to play and she raised her arms making dragon wings of the blue shawl and she smiled at the faces in the summer evening line-up.

Sam the American played. At first the thin soaring notes pleaded. A silly smile settled itself on his face and Sam the American played. Pure notes spun on thin lines up and down and round the evening light glancing off the narrow shafts of late sunlight, spinning round the waiting faces like morning dew-touched cobwebs glistening, silver and jewelled, an amber musician, melting the last of the sunshine, holding it molten in his music while a turquoise girl, a porcelain butterfly, stood swaying in the web of the rhythms holding a cap, catching the moment, holding it still, hearing it linger, soar away thin above the towers, and end.

A brown-skinned man in a turban clapped into the suspended silence and a black woman with tears in her eyes stepped forward and put paper money in the cap.

"Thanks," Angela fell into the velvet compassion of dark eyes. Other people put silver coins into the cap. She walked along the line. She raised her shawl, bowed over one arm to the people, bowed back to Sam the musician, and bowed again. He started the music again. A wild dance. A powerful rhythm. The people moved forward and he played till the line-up had gone round the corner and in through the unseen door. Other people kept coming in twos and threes, hurrying. Sam kept playing with a merry madness and she half danced as she offered the cap to the people. Some of them laughed and put their hands down in purses and pockets, some just looked away.

When the people had almost finished, came only sparsely, Angela pulled the shawl about her and stood a little back to watch the musician. Red musician, amber in the last of the sunlight, with an amber violin, and my mother's peacock lying at your feet—who are you?

He smiled across at her and for a moment made the jig he was roistering come out thin and plaintive and exquisite so it wound inside her and pulled at her tear-strings. She smiled back and the held tears turned porcelain to opals while she began to write in her head another assignment for Mr. Olson. "I watched a street musician and saw the living face of innocence. Mr. Olson, in my head I am always writing assignments. Leaning here against a sooted brick wall, in the last of a London day's sunlight I am watching—the community would say 'a hippy'—a street musician up a grey back-alley, and I think, Mr. Olson, I am listening to a soul winging free, winging wildly to keep summer forever—forever—forever. But there are no butterflies."

The musician broke the spell. "That's about it for tonight," he said, like her father, or Gordon when they'd just tossed the last shovel of muck out of the pig barn.

"I never heard a violin played before," she said. "It seemed very good to me. Are you?"

"Competent." He knelt to pack the violin away in its orange-velvet-lined case.

"Honest. I've never heard big music before. How should I?" she insisted when they had stopped in at his cellar flat to drop off his violin. "Anyhow, how did you?"

"One year, when I was twelve, we had this teacher. A young crazy guy. He caught at my imagination. He started me off, then for years my mother drove me seventy some miles into Shelby for lessons. My poor old Dad! Nearly killed him, the shrieking and the caterwauling when I practised." He laughed. "Funny thing though, once I really started playing, he wouldn't have missed a performance—he even sat through chamber music."

Angela saw vividly a small red-haired boy in a farmhouse like her own practising the violin, very alone, alone for hours, and she was swept with a tenderness for the boy he must have been. Now she looked round his room, a basement low in the ground with a small high window that could only ever catch the passing of feet, patches of damp on the yellowish wall by the window. She was sitting in the one big stuffed chair with her legs under her by a table covered with books and a table lamp made from a green wine bottle, its tall lampshade of rough yellow raffia. Piles of music heaped the floor round the music stand. One extravagance, a large hooked woollen rug like the rays of a wild sunset, oranges and reds and yellows with a surprise of shocking white. He switched on a small electric fire, put the raffia lamp on instead of the overhead, and the room became mellow, home.

And they talked and talked—and talked.

Back in her one-night hotel room her dreams drove out wakefulness and worry, tossed her in a kaleidoscope from Calgary to London; escalators and baggaged peacocks dancing to the music of seagulls catching fire in a lion-legged bathroom where a woman with eyes outlined in cobwebs waved a written page wand from a sunshaft throne and Damion had red hair when he jumped off the spinning double-decker onto the green cobblestones while engines roared and made her sleep late in the romantic brute heart of a foreign city.

Next day they talked and talked again, walked the hot brick back streets and the parks, stood by swans and children feeding them, took great breaths of England, scented blazing flowerbeds, jumped up to touch branches of city-precious trees, and laughed.

Then he waved her goodbye as her train pulled out of the echoing station, leaving his name and his cellar apartment number folded into a sheet of green notepaper, in case you should need me, who knows?

He had given her a bear hug. No strings. Travellers must go light, he had said. Sam the American.

The label she had tied to the handle of the brown suitcase was hanging down from the luggage rack, jigging and twisting on its string to the motion of the train. She was mesmerized by its gyrations in the mirror above the head of the old man who was slumped and dozing in the opposite corner seat; twisting string, twisting label; this side a bright Air Canada sticker stuck on crooked, the other side her own pale printing, lettered such a long time ago on the yellow table at home. The old man's bony veined hands rested on his drawn-up knees and his pink down-edged head had fallen forward, like an embryo. An old embryo. Old man embryo. Embryo.

The dance of the twisting label irritated her, unnerved her. She stood up brusque to herself and rearranged the luggage so it rode firm, the label tucked in. The old man gasped in his doze, then settled again. The passengers in the two other corners by the corridor rode incognito behind newspapers while the train windows rode above the backyards of London-by-the-railway-tracks. Grey, teeming houses and walled welled yards pressed together, black and grey, sometimes a zinc bathtub hung on a wall, sometimes a line of washing flagging down the black, the grey; once a geranium on an upstairs black window ledge, and once a girl sitting on a wall, black wall, girl waving to the train with both hands. Angela waved back and took the yellow-haired smile away on her journey for ever. Girl waving from a backyard wall, travelling as the train gathered speed, rushed past the suburban packaged spread of the sprawling city. London was behind. She hadn't done anything about the abortion.

Then the view from the window was all countryside for hours, a surprise because she had expected an overpopulation of cities stretching from station to station. Instead it was all lush green meadows with dottings of grazing cows that sometimes turned to watch the train go by, and other children waved from grassy places, and there were winding streams and lanes with trees, surprises like the green bubble of calm in a park in the middle of London. It was hard to get back to the thing in her belly that couldn't seem to matter the same now it was away from the censure of home, and she was still high on adventure and travelling towards the sanctuary of wise and protective, loving grandparents.

Her mind travelled to the rhythm of the wheels, soothed and merry, this week to last week, London to home, Damion to Sam, Sam to Damion. Train on a railway track, double track, two trains passing, two track, four track, not so many as the tracks of the mind. Mr. Olson, perceptive, receptive, like you said it should be, the tracks of the mind run simultaneously. Track one the clackety-clack and the old man breathing, track two passing a thatched cottage and a woman on a bicycle, track three is love elastic? is love real? Sam to Damion, Damion, Sam and who other? track four the old man's shoes are worn and polished, does he dream? track five who am I? or am I? shapeless ectoplasm of an unmade soul, clackety-clack, the stations sound hollow. The voices are ghosts with funny accents and when did night fall through the sunset? tunnel over a caterpillar train? What shall I do about the thing in my belly that my mind doesn't want to make a track for? City lights and city lights and out there in the darkness the grandparents will be waiting. Great big beautiful wonderful world.

The grandparents were waiting at the station, two shrunken old people standing close together under the yellow lights, a small pair on the long platform. Grandma Dawson had tied a grey headscarf to cover the tight grey perm of her hair, done new for Angela. She stuck her chin up over the knot of the scarf in belligerent anticipation of the arrival. Grandpa Dawson smoked his cigarette down to the butt, holding it to the last smoke in the ends of his nicotine fingers, peering through the limited space between his hand and the peak of the pulled-down English workingman's cap, breathing sharply, and waiting.

Angela was in the corridor waiting with her baggage by the door and her hair brushed ready. Then she was on the platform standing by her baggage, very bright under the lights in her red and white patterned pantsuit.

"There she is. That's her." The old lady, arms pointing, ran on ahead of Grandpa Dawson and flung herself on Angela and hugged her, then stood at arm's length to survey her, tears running down the wrinkles from underneath the rimless glasses. Grandpa Dawson struggled for breath, stood gasping, looking, dropped his cigarette butt and trod it into the station concrete.

"My, th'art a beauty," he gasped out at last while his rheumy old eyes pushed out a smile. He held out his hand and she squeezed it while her grandmother clung on to her other arm. Angela felt so tall, so big, like a healthy giant dropped among starving children. She kept smiling and didn't know what to say.

"Well, na', don't let's just stand here. Let's get on home." Grandpa took over, bent down wheezingly to pick up some luggage, chose the brown suitcase.

"Oh look," Grandma whimpered, "look, our Dinah's case. The one we bought her to take when she went." The old lady stood pointing with a long finger and tears ran unchecked down her face that suddenly seemed sunken, boneless, shattered. She was trembling, making an emotional show for which Angela was unprepared by habit. She was ill at ease. She adjusted her shoulder bag, picked up her red flight bag and took hold of her grandmother awkwardly with her free arm. "Come on, Grandma. Come on now," she said somehow and steered her along behind the bent grandfather who was leaning dangerously forward under the weight of the old brown case.

A porter tried to persuade them in the hollow empty station to let him call a taxi but Grandfather protested with a big sweep of his arm, "No need for that. No need. It's not that far. We can walk. There's life in us yet, ain't there, me ducks?" he nodded at them and rested the case a minute while he cupped his hands to his face to light up another cigarette.

Grandma squeezed at Angela's arm and pressed her hand. "The buses stop at eleven on our route," she whispered damply, her words flopping an anti-climax at the end of the journey. This was the way it really was. Flat. She was no longer a high-flying pre-paid passenger, in free orbit. She followed the old man into the long palely lit street with the flight bag already hurting her hand and pulling at her shoulder. Their footsteps clicked and echoed between the dark buildings. "I got a new mattress for our Dinah's bed," the strange accent breathing hard at her shoulder told her and Grandfather kept turning round with his cigarette held out at the end of his fingers to say, "Not much farther now," although it was always round another corner and down another alley with herself wondering if she wouldn't have to stop and rest; the flight bag had grown so heavy. She kept saying little bright phrases, trying to sound enthusiastic to the two old people who now had taken possession of her.

"Just round this last corner now. Here we are." They stopped about ten houses along a back alley that seemed to stretch into the city dark endlessly, high, seven or eight foot walls on both sides with wooden doors every few yards set into them. "This is it, look. Number 107." Grandfather worked the heavy latch and pushed the tall door open. In the dark she could just make out the 107 painted pale on the dark door. It opened into a narrow, high-walled L-shaped yard, the length of the L running between the wall that separated the Dawsons' yard from an identical one next door and the projecting back portion of the long thin house itself, one house joined in a long row, one house in a street of houses that ranged its roofs and attic windows like a fortress against the high city sky. One ground-floor window at the very top of the L of the Dawson yard showed a brown light through tight-pulled flowered curtains. "That old man Carter wasting light again. Too senile to know when to go to bed," Grandma grumbled as she stepped ahead across the few yards of the foot of the L to a back door at the end of the house, next to another wall that separated the foot of the L from the foot of the L of the other next-door house. Grandma leaned inside and switched on a light.

"Mind the step," Grandpa wheezed as he stood aside for Angela to go in. "Just follow your grandma, now." She stepped into the closeness of the old house, leaving the built-up town night trapped outside in the walled yard. Green and brown shiny paint on brick walls, brown at the bottom, a black line, then green at the top, and the heavy trapped smell of the wraiths of many meals. A long brown sink and a brick clothes boiler in the first small room. "The scullery," Grandma said and Grandpa gasped behind and put the light out as they went through to the next room. Another steamy brown-and-green-walled small room with a gas stove, a kettle steaming over a low jet. A faint smell of gas. "I'll just make you a nice cup of tea," Grandma was going on, at home now, taking charge. "I left the kettle on specially. Come on in here and take your jacket off. This is the living-room." A high crowded room crushed in between walls of faded but still heavily patterned wallpaper, red roses with swirls of grey and black leaves on a stained white background. A big table filled the centre of the room, dominating with its worn cover of pale puke-green oilcloth. Everything was left ready. Half a loaf of bread turned used side down on the oilcloth, a wooden-handled bread knife lying among the crumbs, a milk bottle half emptied, a glass butter-dish yellow rimmed and greasy, yellow bone-handled knife stuck in the soft of the butter, a brown bowl of white sugar and three cups and saucers, the special ones with red roses, gold leaf, and terribly ornate handles.

"Take your jacket off. Just make yourself at home while I make you a nice cup of tea. You must be ready for a nice cup of tea after all your travelling." Grandmother was busy, bustling. Angela crossed between the table and the assortment of chairs over to the long sweep of a couch that ran under the tall flower-curtained window, the sort of couch she had seen in the show windows of London's antique stores, a slender thing with a curved upholstered back with a thin wooden edge of exquisite carving bending down into richly carved legs. Angela draped her ridiculously bright jacket over the lower arm and sat herself in the deep end that swung up and around like some graceful chariot. She felt too bright for the faded room. She went to move the cushion so she could sit farther back into the deep curve of the couch but stopped herself. The greasy cushion, with silk tassels on the corners, was being used to cover up an assortment of tangled nylon stockings, dark green and grey socks, an apron with its ties tangled in stockings. She patted the cushion back over the mess and leaned against it letting the fingers of one hand feel into the intricacies of the carving on the curved leg of the couch.

Grandpa put the brown case down and hung his coat on a hook behind the stained and varnished brown door. He came and sat in the bulging old armchair opposite her, leaned forward to switch on a bar of the electric fire. "Used to be a proper big fireplace here when your mother was a girl," he told her, pointing to the brown varnished wooden bit of wall where two bars of an electric fire were now attached. "Used to be nice in them days to have a real fire and a kettle singing on the hob. Your mother, our Dinah, used to sit just where you're sitting. She used to tuck her legs under her and read for hours, or draw." He smiled. "We can look at you and fancy we're young again." He leaned back and kept his ancient smile fixed on his granddaughter.

"What do you take in your tea, Dinah? Oh I mean Angela, me duck?" Grandmother stood poised with a white tea-stained china teapot. "Nothing? Ooh Angela. That doesn't seem any way to drink tea. Look, let me just put a little drop of milk in it." She poured some milk in from the bottle, then stirred in a good spoonful of sugar and handed Angela the strong sweet mixture slopping some to drown the roses in the saucer. "Now let me just make you a nice bit of toast," she went on, insistent in her motherliness. "Oh, you've got to eat something," she said when Angela tried to protest she wasn't hungry. "Oh come on, now. There's nothing of you. We need to fill you out a bit. Come on now, have a nice bit of toast with best butter. I always buy best butter." She cut off a slice of bread, holding the loaf against her grey dressed chest, leaning over so the crumbs fell on the green oilcloth. Then she took a long metal fork from a hook on the wall, pronged it into the slice of bread and held it in front of the electric fire until it was striped with brown.

Angela gave in, surrendered herself to the confused little room and to her mother's parents. She sipped at the strong tea and balanced the slopping saucer on her knee and looked from one to the other of her grandparents, trying to find some trace of her mother, of home. She put the saucer onto the table and put her legs up under her. Grandpa Dawson pushed his cigarette butt into his swilling saucer and his old face lit up again. "Ah, I can't get over it," he said softly, fondly. "You sit there just like my girl, our Dinah." And in his smile, in the tilt of his head, Angela imagined she sensed a ghost of her mother.

"But you're fairer. And those eyes don't belong in our family," Grandma said, pausing with the butter knife poised over the slice of toast in her hand to look at her shrewdly. "Is your Dad fair? We never saw him, you know. I'd a given him a piece of my mind if I had. Going and marrying a kid like that. He was old enough to know better. Old enough to be her father. I'd a liked to have killed him."

Angela watched the bitterness in her grandmother's suspicious old face and watched the butter going thick on the toast. "Were you as blonde as me, Grandma?" she asked to change the atmosphere. The butter-thick greasy toast was in her hand now and she felt out of place, as though she had got trapped in a late-night old English movie.

"You bet she was a fair one." Grandfather spoke in indulgently, soothingly, fondly. "Nobody fairer and prettier than my old dutch." He stretched out to put his hand on his wife's waist and give her a swift hug. Angela looked away down to the butter dripping in yellow gobs onto her hand, finding the to and fro of raw feelings hard to take.

"I was all right till our Dinah put years on me, her never coming back." The old lady was whining like keening, swaying as she stood by the table. "It was that man marrying her as put these wrinkles on my face, that and losing my boy. Put the grey hairs in my head, they did. Our Dinah never coming back. I'll never forgive that man to the day I die. After us raising a beautiful girl like our Dinah. More tea, duck?" she suddenly changed her tune, livened up.

"The girl must be tired, it's the early hours," Grandpa reminded the old woman. "Why don't you show her our Dinah's room. You've got a whole two months for talking. Plenty of time for talking."

He gasped behind them lugging the brown suitcase when Grandma shushed them along a dark narrow corridor to the bottom of the wide staircase. "Ssh. Don't make a noise or I shall get complaints galore tomorrow. Everybody's in bed, except old man Carter. He'll be fidgetin' to know who's here. Nosy old bugger." Grandmother's stage whisper kept on along the corridor and up the three flights of stairs to the third landing. "Our Dinah's room. Never changed a thing. Except I bought a new mattress. A good one. Never let her room out to anyone. Not even when we could have made good money with it. We've never let her room out, not even when we ran the house like a proper hotel and had nice clean people in it. Different it was then to what it is now. Just rooms for old people. Nobody else wants rooms like this now, except old people whose children have left them."

"Here you are." She pushed open the door. "Same as the day she left it, except for the new mattress."

They all three of them stood just inside the door of Dinah's room. Grandfather pushed the brown case over by the large mahogany wardrobe and held up his face to be kissed good-night. "Goodnight. God bless," he said and she hugged him round his old shoulders and touched her lips to his old cheek. " 'Night, Grandpa. Sleep well."

"Come on, Doris. Let the girl get to bed; she's had a long day," he said taking his little wife by the arm. Angela gave her a hug and pecked her. Then she was alone . . . arrived in her sanctuary, in her mother's room.

Angela stood just inside the door by her red flight bag on the worn, once blue, now grey linoleum, and looked around the tall oblong room with a high ceiling that was a grey-white above the yellow bare bulb, walls that once had had blue wallpaper, now a pale faded design of blue Chinamen in blue coolie hats dancing under a blue yoke with two dancing buckets. So pale a room, almost a ghost of a room, so faded, the mahogany wardrobe and dressing table large monsters in the cloud of paleness. The patchwork bedspread, a strange irregular pattern, was a memory of reds and pinks and oranges, a faint gentle memory spread out between the rail head and foot boards, of the same heavy, forbidding mahogany. One pale ornament, a blue and grey and pink shepherdess, stood on the dressing table to be reflected in the tilt of the mirror, a lady in a lacy bonnet in a frilly swirl of skirt. One small rug by the bedside to break the grey chill of the linoleum. It seemed to be made of looped, frayed string and a pattern set in it with bright yellow and orange rags, a bright yellow sunflower to catch bare feet coming from warm bed to a cold floor. It had stayed bright. The brightest thing in the room. Along the wall under the tall narrow window there was a row of bookshelves made from rough apple boxes, crammed with books and papers and things that would have been her mother's. Angela shuddered, tried to think of her own private room, with the scent of hyacinths creeping under the door. How would it be to have someone else, a stranger, moving into her privacy. Who would move into her room someday if she never went back home?

It was cold. She decided to unpack in the morning. Now she took out the big red nightgown her mother had warned her she would need in English bedrooms, and got into it quickly and opened the wardrobe door to hang up her pantsuit. Brown wood scent, dense, clung inside the dark of the big wardrobe and she saw herself in the mirror on the inside of the door, her reflection hanging in the heavy wood scent with her mother's expression on her face. She shrugged and frowned at herself, hung up her clothes, closed the wood scent and the reflection away in the dark and felt the linoleum strike cold through her bare feet. She climbed into the bed, between the patched grey-white sheets under the faded quilt, pushed her feet to the chill depths. They touched warmth. She investigated the warm shape with her feet, then fished the fat rubber hot-water bottle up and hugged it to her red nightie. Love is putting a hot-water bottle in your granddaughter's bed! She nestled her feet on the warm patch the hot-water bottle had made and she lay flat with the comforting thing in her arms. Damn. She had to get out of bed to put out the light.

Hugging the warm rubber bottle she put the light out at the switch by the door, went over and opened the curtains, looked down into the black backyards and from them to the faraway stars in the narrow high sky. The grey light of an industrial city fell between the roofs into her window, into her mother's room, her room now.

Then she crept back into the bed with its new mattress and closed her mind, willing herself into the tiredness of an empty sleep. Empty. Empty.

While the house still slept, Angela lay warm in the bed under the faded patchwork cover and heard the strange city clatter into daylight. Heavy boots rang down the back alley and gates banged. Voices called messages through the grey, and morning came light over the silhouette of the tall house roofs on the other side of the alley. How closed in it was! How near, how strange the nearness of so many voices, talking, calling, saying goodbye. Somewhere bottles rattled. For a long time the house itself was quiet, all the voices and noises outside; people who had to go to early morning work moving. No one in the house of old people had to be up for work. Angela lay with her hands warm on her belly, thinking.

That wasn't the way she had thought of her grandparents. The blue airletters hadn't seemed like the people who sent them. Perhaps the airletters were the words of the people they wanted to be, the people who had never been able to get out any other way. And grandparents! She had had her own myth. Grandparents, mellow people, secure, calm and kindly, a very present help in trouble. Angela turned her face into the pillow to obliterate the memory of her fantasy, the cosy dream of a fairy-tale grandmother lovingly taking charge, understanding and forgiving in her great wisdom. She pressed her face hard into the pillow. There was no oasis. And she had committed herself to two months here. Nine weeks now. Plus two months. She pressed her hands into her belly, measured that the pelvic bones still stood up above the flesh. If she were home she would get up and run across the pasture. If this were home birds would be waking. Instead in the room next door an old man was coughing, hacking and coughing. In a room above somebody was thumping around. A toilet flushed. Other people coughing. Somebody somewhere filled a kettle, the water hitting the hollow tin then filling. Footsteps moved about the house. She lay still, not knowing what her part was in the house. Should she get up or wait till all the others had finished with the bathrooms? She felt as though she had to hide under the bedclothes, her belly behind her hands.

Then came the food smells. Toast burning. Bacon. Was somebody frying strong fish? Grease smells that made her remember gobs of oozing yellow butter. The sickness came again and she couldn't hold it back, had to rush out to the bathroom, across the landing and down a long narrow passageway, windows at one side, rooms at the other. She ran along the cold linoleum corridor holding her long red nightie about her, got into the vast old bathroom and latched the bolt on the bathroom door before she retched and vomited last night's tea and yellow butter into the time-crazed, brown-crusted, neglected toilet bowl. Her retchings echoed and magnified in the cavernous bathroom, then she stood with her forehead against the frosted glass of the window, saw, through a hole where the brown cracks met, down into the house next door, into a room with a bare light bulb, a table crowded with dishes, the room across the black backyard next door that corresponded with the Dawsons' living-room. A view through a cracked window into the thin backyards, across the blackened brick dividing wall into another house. Suddenly she was cold. Her feet were bare.

Why hadn't she brought a towel? She washed her hands and face with the hard soap and tried to wipe them on stiff toilet paper and shivered. It was cold. She must remember to put slippers on. She hugged herself to go along the corridor.

The door to the room next to the bathroom opened as she came to it and a yellow-skinned face peered round the door, an old face with thin yellow-white hair scraggled in metal curlers. The top half of the body came round the door in a blue woollen dressing-gown held together across a concave chest by a veined yellow hand.

"Are you all right, me duck? I couldn't help but hear you being so sick and all."

Angela stopped and pulled herself up tall with her two hands flat across her belly. "Oh," she hedged politely, "I must have eaten something."

The old woman came all the way out of the doorway, holding it pulled to behind her and clutching the grease-stained dressing-gown in the other hand. She looked up at Angela from among a network of wrinkles. "Ooh. I know," the voice was like a wise little girl's. "You must be Doris's granddaughter, all the way from Canada. You all right, eh? You sure?"

"Sure. Sure." Angela said but felt pale seeing the wise old bird's eyes prying her naked, tearing her to a little size. "Who are you?" she asked to break the pierce of the old scrutiny.

"Me. I'm Madeleine. Miss Madeleine Crookshank. I've rented this room for over ten years now. After your mother's time. Your mother did very well for herself, did all right for herself in Canada, eh?"

Angela shivered. "You bet she did," she said and tried to move away.

"I reckon she did. People talk about her round here. Reckon she did very well for herself, Doris says. You all right, eh?" The eyes looked knowingly over Angela, peered up into her face. "You don't look right to me. You've got a funny little look. Sure you're all right, eh?"

"I'm cold. I must get some slippers on," Angela rushed away with a sort of wave backwards and she felt the old eyes watching her go. She got back into the cold bed and tried to get warm again. That woman. That poor grotesque along the landing. She knew. She knew that funny little look. The bed wouldn't warm up again to give solace, so she got up in the chill room. She belted a loose blue dress in tightly with a wide red belt, two notches too tight to prove it could be done, and she stood by the window to braid her hair, one thick braid over one shoulder, and while she was braiding it she looked down into the black-tiled backyards at the bottom of the grey morning. But—a tree.

One tree, and it in the Dawson backyard, right at the end by the gate where she had come in last night. She must have walked right past it last night, and it a biggish tree, reaching out over the wall, spreading its branches, and bunches of purple berries among the still leaves. The only tree in the backyards as far as she could see. Hardly a sign of life. A woman sitting outside on a high window ledge, leaning out and backwards to clean the window. A window like the one in Angela's room. Angela struggled with the rusted catch halfway up her

74

window, forced it round with her farm-girl's strong fingers, then pushed and strained to move the bottom of the window up. It resisted. Closed shut for nineteen years. She battled with it until it went up suddenly with a thump rough enough to shake the house. As though from nowhere a sparrow hovered outside and, wanting to claim it, she rummaged down in her peacock shoulder bag for the packet of peanuts her father had insisted he buy her at Calgary airport when he wanted to send her away with everything she could ever need. She tore the cellophane wrapping now with her teeth and crumbled some of the greasy nuts and spread them on the soot-blackened window ledge. She pulled the window down again and watched two sparrows land in. City sparrows.

"Did I hear you up?" Grandmother Dawson peered round the door. "I thought I heard you but I didn't know but what you'd want to sleep in. I've got the kettle on. Come on down and let's you and me have a nice cup of tea."

In daylight the house seemed big and interesting, its staircase a splendid construction to look down through the layers of the house, down to the patterned tiles of the front entrance hall. The handrail felt good and solid, time polished, and the light coming in to the central hallway came with a glow through the stained-glass windows of the front door. Really it had once been a splendid house, Angela realized as she followed like a giant behind her little shrivelled grandmother, past the doors on every landing with faint noises of a life behind them and the whiff of breakfast hanging associated with each name label slotted into a metal holder on each heavily varnished brown door. How the grandmother talked! Non-stop! "When our Dinah was a little girl we ran a proper hotel with meals and service. Had two regular maids then. And the lodgers. None of your old folk then. No sir! Real ladies and gents. Actors and musicians. The war changed all that. Still we can't complain; the place keeps us in our old age. Some people have their children to look out for them. Not us! We weren't that lucky. But we've got the house."

On and on she went, information peppered with innuendo. Angela sat up to the table on the side by the two glowing bars of the electric fire and practised a vague smile for each whine and innuendo. She was beginning to get the pattern of complaint in the old woman's thinking. Her habit of thinking. The old woman sat facing her sideways to the table, and the warmth and the closed-in-ness was almost cosy. Angela was facing the window, looking out across the bread and the milk bottle, over the elegant line of the couch, to a view of a blackened brick wall. Morning strained in over the house she had looked into through the crack and hole in the bathroom window, and shone in grey pools on the green oilcloth.

"I leave your grandpa, my old Harry, in bed. He's not well, you know. I have to look after him if I'm to keep him with me." The kindly grandmother talking who lovingly put the hot-water bottle in the bed. "Broke his heart too when our Dinah never came back. Her marrying an old man with no family nor nothing."

Angela thought of her father hefting her up onto her horse when she was still a girl and fishing at the lake with her and her brother and she had to protect him. She smiled, gently she hoped. "He wasn't so old," she said, "and a very kind man."

"Don't you talk to me about him," her grandmother pulled in her mouth and spoke sourly. "No family. Nothing. Somebody's cast-off child. Most likely a no-good girl's who never knew who the father was. That's the story behind half the poor little bastards as get brought up in orphanages. Poor little buggers. But I sure as hell didn't raise my Dinah to marry a man like that."

Angela bit into her dry toast. She had made it herself and managed to do without the butter. She closed her eyes a moment against the welling anger and she breathed hard to keep it down the way she had fought her nausea. Learn to let the old woman talk, repeat the same message again and again, like her father himself swaddling his every kindness in prejudice. Grandmother was happy just to go on talking, talking out her own show. She asked very little about Canada, or even about her Dinah. And if she did ask she never waited for an answer, interrupted to tell her own memories and wrap them in her own grievances. Grievances. Grievances.

Soon she had brought out old envelopes stuffed with old photographs and was spreading them among the crumbs on the table; photographs of herself and Grandpa when they were young, of Chris and Dinah through all the stages. A Canadian photograph of Chris in his uniform outside the Parliament Buildings in Ottawa. Dinah always the same fair, serious, straight-nosed child; with a big teddy bear; with the little boy Jeffrey from down the alley. Dinah and Jeffrey standing by their bikes when they were in grammar school.

"He's done very well, Jeffrey has, and he wasn't a patch on our Dinah. He plays with a big orchestra, in London. We see him on the telly sometimes. Never know what our Dinah might have done, might have amounted to something. My, how we lived to regret the day we ever let her take that trip—to broaden her mind." She shook her head and clucked and filled up the teapot again.

Angela studied the school photograph of her mother with the bikes and Jeffrey. Grandmother was going on again about the silly family Dinah stayed with who encouraged her into marriage to that Joe Moynahan, the same old things over and over. "My mother said I should get a bike," Angela interrupted the flow while she put her dishes together to take out to the scullery.

"Well, I wouldn't be surprised if our Dinah's bike isn't down in the shed at the bottom of the yard. Your granddad'll have to look at it for you, then you'll be able to get out a bit. Our Dinah used to ride off into the country and come back with flowers. She always brought us flowers. Sometimes autumn leaves. But the bluebells, I remember, I can smell them now."

Angela listened and nodded, kept a vague smile ready for the moment when she would have to shut off. She wondered if she dare wipe the crumbs off the table, then decided against it. Where could she put the crumbs? It was hard to know what to do in a strange house. She put the photographs back in the envelopes. "Maybe I should go out and look around," she said, trying to find a way to break away into her own day. Grandmother said she should go and introduce herself at Tunnicliffe's, the bakers where she was going to work, just up the street, then go and have a look around.

Pulling back the bolts of the front door, like bolts of a dungeon, Grandmother let Angela out onto the high steps of the entranceway to the house, stood a moment to point the way to the baker's, then closed the door, and Angela heard the bolts being slid home and the chain jangling.

77

She stood on the stone steps for a moment to survey the narrow main road of her mother's childhood with its red double-deckers and dashing vans and roaring motorbikes and little flitting cars. The sidewalks were already moving with women pushing baby carriages and older women loaded with baskets and shopping bags, plodding shapelessly.

Thursday morning. This time last week she had been writing her last exam, impatient to get away. What a lot had happened in one week. A shaft of sunlight broke through across the street making the shoppers the more drab, the more darkly shapeless.

Angela pressed her arm against the warm texture of the peacocks on her bag and wished she had worn a coat; English sunshine was only cool this morning. She braced herself and walked slowly down the steps and walked slowly up the street on the side where the sun shone. Eventually she would have to cross over into the shade to get to Tunnicliffe's, the bakery pressed between a tobacconist's and an art-needlework store. The scents of new bread and sugary cookies came across the street from the shade into the sun where she stood and spied on the goings-on in the shop before she plucked up courage, and enough cool and composure to let another experience swamp her, sweep her like a forlorn crumpled cake bag down the gutter of another day. Another day, going. She had to count the days.

A toddler with rosy cheeks dived into the bag his mother had stuck in at the bottom of the baby carriage, pulled out a jammy tart, let the empty bag fall, blow away, while he bit into the crumbling pastry, sticky red all over him; a slap from his mother; the baby bleating, a puling cry coming across the traffic. The red-faced woman behind the counter laughing all the time, shaking three red chins and a big bosom inside a voluminous overall. She must be Beaty Tunnicliffe, "as was Beaty Johnson," Grandmother said, "Beaty Johnson as went to school with our Dinah, that is till our Dinah got the scholarship and went to

78

the other school. Our Dinah was the clever one." Beaty Tunnicliffe with her red face and frazzled dun hair never seemed to
stop laughing and the customers came out smiling.

"Now don't tell me," she laughed when Angela went in the
moment nobody else was there. "Now don't tell me. Dinah
Dawson's little girl. I'd have known you anywhere, got the
same look."

Tunnicliffe's was a different world again, fat and jolly. Behind the shop there was a big bread-warm bakehouse, vast
ovens deep in the walls at one side and shelves round the other
three laden with breads and cakes galore. Steve, Beaty's big
balding husband, ran the bakehouse assisted by Mike, a young
chirpy guy with his long hair fastened back under a hairnet.
He whistled when Beaty took Angela in. "Wowee. Some new
cookie," he quipped and looked her over appraisingly. Everybody quipped and laughed. It was infectious. She stayed long
enough to drink tea with them at the white scrubbed table in
the corner of the bakehouse, to be introduced to a dozen customers. "You remember Dinah Dawson. Angela, her daughter
all the way from Canada." They laughed and joked all the time
and it was restoring, made her feel like somebody in her own
right again, "Angela from Canada". Rita was the other assistant
in the shop, a pert bottle-blonde with the tiniest edge of red
skirt showing under her short white smock. She prattled to
every customer, called them all duck. That was hard to get used
to, everybody being called duck. Although, how soon a new
situation became normal! In less than an hour she had met
Beaty, Steve, Mike, and Rita; got the feel of them; learned how
the money-till worked; learned the names of a dozen sorts of
iced and decorated, sugar-coated, raisin-filled confections; become familiar with the smell and sound of bakehouse and till-
ringing shop. It seemed as though it could be a fun place for
two months, the two months while Beaty ("Call me Beaty," she
laughed, "everybody does") was away in Australia with her
daughter who had emigrated there. "Just worked in right, your
coming has. Our Shirley is due to have her baby three weeks
from now. I'm not going to let her be there among strangers
without her mother. A girl needs her mother at such a time,"
Beaty laughed good-naturedly. "But I'll be around here till Wed-

nesday, so if there's anything you need, my girl, just you call out for Beaty. That's me. Always on call, me!" Angela believed her, the big good-natured woman who seemed so much older than her own mother, and spilled her goodwill into the morning so that Angela left to explore the streets ready to walk on air again, swing along in the sunshine side of the streets, laughing at the working boys who whistled after her. Angela the Canadian. She felt good again. She took off her wide red belt and swung it round on her little finger as she jaunted from grey street to grey street, breathing in the feel of her mother's city. Houses, row on row, without tree or garden, their front doors opening right off the sidewalk and children teeming out of open doors with the smells of urine and cabbage. The dry, dusty brick smell she remembered from London, a lifetime of two days ago with Sam the American. Poor streets and wealthy streets. One wide street with painted and polished houses, a few steps up to each door, white net over all the windows, brass polished name plates at every door. A row of doctors. She walked up and down the street twice, then back again, reading the polished names. A large woman with shoes and stockings that looked as though they belonged to a nurse took a key from her black bag and opened her way into one of the houses. The woman had grey hair, short and wiry.

Angela waited to gather courage, then she knocked the polished brass knocker onto the polished doorplate, and tried to think of words to say when the person opened the door. She could hear the feet coming heavily but muffled from somewhere inside. Then the woman was there with the door open, standing two steps high above her and looking down at her out of a hard face with agate eyes as though Angela were one of the urine-smelling back-street children—and because the eyes looked at her that way, she was. Angela uncomfortable on one leg, hesitant, stumbling for words to answer the sharp inquiry from the thin lips.

"Mr. MacDougal is not here till three." It was patronizing and final in an accent she knew to be Scottish. She tried to say something, make a plea, but the words were garbled, she felt so inadequate and displaced.

The bleak, set face rebuked her. "Do you have a recommendation from your own doctor? Mr. MacDougal sees no one without a recommendation."

"But . . . How . . ."

The woman said a firm, unsmiling "Good day," and the door closed, leaving Angela silly and snubbed on the step. Nobody. But she had to try. Thursday. She started work on Monday. She had to try. She let her despair drive her out of the polished brass-plated street, farther into the labyrinth of narrow streets and poverty, with half-clothed children running everywhere, little boys with bulging bellies under shrunken jerseys, bare bottoms and genitals exposed for want of pants; women sitting slumped on doorsteps or leaning with folded arms cushioning flabby breasts. All the women of the world pregnant, bulging down the back streets of the soiled and teeming city. Cows. With dead hair, and voices that squall at their children, and hands that hit out, and words that shout obscenities. Angela walked on the shadowy side to become invisible, walked down one street behind two slow women who leaned back over the uneven hems of their belly-hoisted skirts, skirts revealing grey, tired flesh of sagging thighs and volcanoes of varicose veins. She bent her head and walked slowly behind them not wanting to pass, not wanting to follow. When they turned into an open doorway that went from the street into a large house, she read the dull brass plaque on the door which named a Dr. Joan Donovan, and a notice on a card hung by string on a nail driven into the door frame announced, "Thursday Clinic, 10 a.m. to 2.30 p.m." She went down the dark corridor after the pregnant women and through another open door into a waiting-room with leather-covered benches round the sides and sat just inside the door, not sure it was the right place to come, nor what right she had to be there in a strange city.

She was the only woman there without a swollen belly. Even the girl with a baby on her knee was swollen again, or perhaps she had never gone down. Seven women sitting waiting with their hands across their bellies, except for the one who held the small child. Seven women first, then Angela. After a while of waiting a nurse came in from down the corridor. "Have I got all your urine samples?" she asked looking round at them all. "You," she paused over Angela, "a new girl, eh?" She was cheerful, very young, pleasantly aggressive. "Come on," she said. "Let's get your particulars and a sample." Angela followed her into the room down the corridor, and not knowing what else to do allowed herself to be entered on a form and allowed herself to be sent into a toilet with a jar to provide a urine sample. She felt powerless, caught up in a warm undertow, ridiculous and violated peeing into such a small jar. She found herself half-laughing in the toilet without a catch, trying to hold the door and aim into the little aperture, wondering how the fat stiff women managed. The nurse was cheerful, impersonal, matter of fact, and was already involved with two other women before Angela was finished with. But, at last, she was in a place that dealt with women and she was going in to see Doctor Joan Donovan, whoever she was. But she was a woman and would therefore understand, would tell her what to do.

Angela felt calm, almost elated, as she watched the world of pregnant women around her. She was too gay, too bright, too thin for the dreary waiting-room. She looked with affection, with satisfaction at her long, bare, sun-browned feet in her brief sandals, and the long stretch of her ankles, unveined, not like the other women's.

She thought smugly, Mr. Olson, see, I am doing something about it, being positive, and soon enough. I am seeing to it soon enough and next year I can come back.

She was glad for herself. Just one day in a new city, and she was coping! She thumbed through the tatty magazines full of love stories with romantic flowing illustrations, interrupted with ads for feeding bottles and diapers, and with articles and recipes for making ends meet, everywhere in the pages laughing women backed by square-jawed men.

She wasn't part of this room of women, she thought, watching them, a spectator, patient as one by one the women went in and came out, while others came in and filled up the black stridulant benches with their bodies.

At last, after more than an hour, it was her turn and she was sitting opposite Doctor Joan Donovan, an elderly woman with a lined, tired face, attentive kindly eyes. She looked from Angela to the form the nurse had put before her on the table between them. "You're not native to these parts?" she asked as though time were long and there were no one else waiting in the still-full waiting-room. "How nice Canada sounds. You must find it very different here." She passed her hands over her face as though to wipe the district off and offer herself with unreserve to the bright face opposite her. Woman to able woman across the table. Angela sat up out of her waist and met the mind across the table with a smile that confirmed an equality. This is my sort of woman, she thought, like the woman on the plane. "I want an abortion," she said. "Soon. I am nine weeks pregnant."

The eyes across the table did not waver but registered distress and sympathy. The doctor reached out her hand as though to touch the girl, but she only picked up a small model of a uterus and vagina, which tilted and turned on a plastic stand, and toyed with it.

"That's a pretty drastic request," she said smiling. "Tell me about it." She was very gentle.

"I didn't mean to have a baby. It was a mistake."

Angela spoke very clearly, very matter of factly, because with the professional woman there, smiling, it all seemed so simple, so matter of fact. "I just came to travel for a year, then next year I plan to go to university."

"How nice," the doctor smiled still, but sadly, and passed one hand over her face, the other still tilting the plastic uterus. "So you're not married?"

"Oh no. No, NO." The reply came out too vehemently, and she moved her eyes from the questioning eyes of the doctor to look into the crisp short curls of the greying brown hair, strong hair and natural.

"I gather you don't want to be married?"

"No. Not at all."

"I see." She looked away down to the hands on the model. "I see." The voice sighed and was very professional. "Do you know who the father is?" She said it slowly and smiled down at her hands, no panic, no censure. As Mr. Olson said, she will not moralize. It is just her job. But something in Angela recoiled and she hardened her eyes. "I am not promiscuous," she retorted, and was on the defensive, not equal any more.

The doctor looked up at her again and still smiled, spoke very softly, with professional patience, "Then what about the father?" So kind. So patient. So practised. "Does he want to marry you?"

Angela recoiled again, bit her lip and looked down at her hands resting on her bare thighs, and she nodded her head from side to side, not hiding some anguish.

"You didn't answer me." Professionally firm. "Does he want to marry you?"

"I've never thought about it." The words were wrung from her, and honest. She had never thought what he wanted. Poor Gordon. "No. No. I don't want to marry him."

"But you are having his baby. You must have wanted him at some time." The voice was so soft, so very patient. The eyes still smiled offering calm and reassurance.

Angela forced herself to hold the woman's gaze. "No," she said as though she were an intelligent woman speaking to an equal again. "You just don't understand."

"Perhaps. Perhaps," the woman was soothing, professional, not equal, denied the moment of mind to mind. But she watched the girl carefully, courteously placating. "Well, let me have a look at you," she said, businesslike. "Take all your clothes off and just hop up onto the couch over there," she pointed to the general area of a screen on wheels.

Behind the screen Angela draped her dress over her underwear and her peacock bag on the one wooden chair and she pulled the small sheet over her nakedness as she lay back on the crinkling paper-covered couch and looked at the yellow patterns of stain in the high ceiling. If she closed her eyes she could go to sleep, give way to the unutterable weariness of her pregnant mind. She could hear the doctor washing her hands, then she came in pulling on a rubber glove.

"Now just relax," she said encouragingly, brightly. "Now put your feet, your heels up here," she motioned to wide-set metal stirrups at the bottom of the couch and everything in Angela recoiled. She hated herself. The loss of privateness. But she did as she was told and breathed deeply to fight against her silly proud feeling that now, this moment, was the worst of all. She had lost everything. The cold gloved hand pushed up inside her and the other hand bore down on the belly, pushing, probing, feeling, and the doctor very businesslike kept saying, "Fine. Now just relax. Fine. Fine." She wasn't Angela. She was like the model on the desk, a tipped uterus at the end of a vagina. She watched the ceiling and hardened her eyes.

"Okay. You can put your legs down." The doctor pursed her lips, looked at the body, lunged forward and squeezed the breasts with a cold hand. "Fine," she murmured. "Fine. Just splendid. Okay, put your clothes on and come and talk to me," then she was washing her hands again on the other side of the screen.

Angela brushed her hair out free before she went out again and shook it round her face to make her feel feminine again, human, or was it to use as a veil? She rubbed some creme sachet into her hands like hand cream to take away the smell of medical lubricant and doctors, made the surgery loud with To a Wild Rose.

Doctor Joan Donovan was sitting at the table again, her elbow on it, and she was holding up a prescription slip, smiling kindly, patiently out of her older woman's well-lined face. Angela sat down and looked at the woman hopefully, her hands clenched in her lap. The doctor leaned nearer and smiled kindly. Her eyes were tired inside the faded blue.

"Now let us think what we are going to do, what the alternatives are." She spoke with considered reasonableness, but not to an equal, to somebody who had to be organized, put on track, a child. "If you stay here I can take your case. Later—if you like, we have a very good home for unmarried mothers I could recommend you to and you could have your baby in the small hospital there."

85

Angela felt that the chair was swimming under her but she kept her eyes fixed on the professional woman while her insides crawled. She sucked in her cheeks and kept all expression out of her eyes, while anger tore at her throat.

"You could go back and marry that young man." The voice was coaxing, soothing for a child. "You are an extremely attractive young woman—I feel sure he would want to marry you." Words caressing to stroke the head, to make the world come right and good. "It is his child too, you must remember. It is a little life you accepted into you, you know."

Blood roared through Angela's head and she held the edges of the chair seat, clenched hard to hurt her knuckles and kept her eyes without expression, found the turned-off look her mother wore. She felt very silly, very violated, and suddenly very proud. She shook her head and let go with her hands. So, she had been reprimanded, put in her place. Nobody. A pregnant nobody. A naughty girl.

"Now be a good sensible girl. Make sure you're eating well for baby's sake."

"But I don't want a baby." Christ, why did she say that? Why did she let the words out?

"You'll feel differently in a little while, in another month, you'll see, my dear. You'll cope. You'll see, there's always room for a baby. And if you really don't want to keep him—we can arrange to put him out for adoption. It is a precious life, you know."

What could she say. She wasn't anybody. Not an equal woman at all. Just a silly pregnant naughty girl. As she turned to leave the doctor pressed the prescription in her hand, a tonic to tide her over, and a reminder to drink plenty of milk and orange juice, and bring a urine sample next time she came a month from today. "And if you have any problems don't hesitate to come back any time."

Angela tossed her head and raised her chin as she walked through the still-crowded waiting-room of mothers, and she let her hair fall forward as she broke out from the dark corridor of the house into the sunshine. God I tried. I tried again. She felt full but empty, so bursting with anger that she reeled drunk on emptiness. She walked. Endless black pavement. She walked and could not get away. Endless pavement. Endless crowding houses imprisoning her with her certainty that her last chance was gone. She had to have a baby. Endless houses with women on the steps. Women bulging and drab, their breasts hunched up on folded arms. Endless drab. Never a tree. No grass. She wanted to cry to tear her anger out, or scream against the crowding bricks, crowding black pavement.

But where do you go to scream? Where are there no women watching on the steps? Where is there a place to scream? Where do you go? To scream?

At an intersection of crowding streets there was a public lavatory with a stone Queen Victoria sitting on top of the bricks and stone. Angela fled under the dome of Queen Victoria, found a penny, struggled it into the slot, let herself into a fouled, brown-tiled cubicle; stench vile. In between vomits she tore the prescription into small pieces and flushed them away with somebody else's diarrhoeic stools and her own vomit.

The sun wilted on the other side of the street when she wandered unwillingly back to the gateway marked 107. She pushed the heavy gate open and put off the moment of leaving the light of the late afternoon to go into the closeness of the house. The late sun touched the top of the city tree and cast trembling dapples through it onto the black tile of the yard. The leaves and berries were pungent green among the closed-in bricks. At some time a rockery had been built up in the corner against the high wall where the tree was planted. Angela climbed up the rocks and hoisted herself onto the wall top, to sit among the lower branches, her face dappled with the leaves, and she looked down the narrow back alley, black, city geometric, edges sharp with shadows. Far down the alley, the sun lit on the edges of some other tree, just leaf edges, no branches crossing the wall as here from her grandmother's yard. If only she could sit in the branches and hold time off.

Was it only this morning that she first saw the tree? Only last night that she first came through this gate in the high wall? What a long time ago it seemed that the old men were coughing and Madeleine in the rag of a blue dressing-gown had eyed her. How far away! She glanced up through the tree to find the window of her room where this morning she had put out Calgary peanuts for city sparrows. One day, that was all it had taken, and this city was her own; it was so long ago when the two sparrows came, before today's sun had broken through the level smoke of the morning sky.

"Penny for 'em?" The old voice came up softly from underneath and she smiled because the tone was caressing. "Penny for the thoughts under that fair head," Grandpa eased her from her reverie, looking up with his wrinkles pulled into a smile and the inevitable cigarette burning away in his fingers.

"Hi Grandpa," she said gently, why gently she didn't know except that that was the way it seemed right to speak to him.

"Just like your mother. Our Dinah used to perch up there."
He looked up at her with unabashed love and she had to sit
still to hold it gently in the fragrance of the leaves. "But my!
We thought we must 'a lost you, you've been out and away so
long. Your grandma's been all of a dither worrying about you.
She's kept your dinner warm. And see here," he leaned round
into the lowest and nearest bit of the house that Grandma
called the shed and he led out the bike with its faded brown
wicker basket on the handlebars. "See here," he smiled from it
to her, "all fixed up. You go and try it out after you've eaten
your dinner, eh," his voice coaxed and caressed her as she
wheeled the oiled and polished bike up and down the yard.
"See, all it needed was new tires." Then Grandma was calling
from the door and she had to go in to the smell of her own
dinner that had been kept warm between two plates over a pan
of water on a low gas jet in the kitchen. Stew and mashed
potatoes brown with gravy and dark cabbage, heavy and wet.
Grandma brushed the crumbs aside and moved the loaf of
bread over, then sat down to watch Angela eat the food. So wet.
She picked at it and tried to disguise her revulsion because her
grandmother had put it before her like a gift, but, when the old
lady went out to the kitchen to make the tea, Angela managed
to pull her peacock bag to her from the carved couch and, like
a thief, fork a good part of the meal into the tissues she had
brought from her own bedroom, packed that last morning on
the farm. A sog of cabbage, grisly meat and gooey brown
potato pushed down and hidden between the peacocks!

As soon as it seemed decent to leave she went out and practised riding the bike up and down the lesser used streets, stayed
out until it was almost dark, then when she did have to come in
she made an excuse that she was tired and got away to hide in
the pale bedroom.

The hot-water bottle was already down in her bed, placed
with love, just in the right place for her feet.

So—she had this room and a bicycle. Escapes. At night she
could pull the curtains with their faded pink roses across the
window and sit on the small mat with the sunflower on it,
wrapped in the warm things her mother had made her bring
for English bedrooms; she could sit over by the apple-box book-

cases and read through her mother's old schoolbooks, and write in the exercise book that was to be her journal the assignments for herself that might have been thought out for Mr. Olson. Mr. Olson, the thoughts have become very mundane. Like how to creep along a passage without being seen by old men, and how to get into the bathroom before Madeleine hears me coming and wants to talk while she fills her kettle and looks me over for signs. The hardest is how to eat Grandmother's soggy, kept-warm meals, or how to get enough of it into my bag to flush down the toilet later. If I don't eat can I keep my stomach in for the two months I have to stay? Except for not eating I try not to think of the thing in my belly that I know I am now committed to. My mind knows it is there but I refuse to believe it. . . . My mother's books frighten me. Now I know from them the work of Gauguin. Not only him. Others. Kandinski and Chagall and Brueghel who painted a wedding dance. Not like my wedding dances! I found an essay my mother had written about El Greco. The teacher had written "Excellent" at the end of it and my mother wrote about the elongated emotions of the artist soaring like the notes of a plaintive violin reaching for joy. It is weird, disturbing, to wonder what your mother did with her thoughts.

There is never any hot water and the bathroom is very cold and I try to muffle the noise in there so Madeleine won't know I'm there and be waiting. I have to smuggle my washing out to a laundromat because Grandma thinks I change my clothes too often—and wash my hair too often.

Behind the wardrobe I found a large art binder, just as my mother had left it. I bought some thumbtacks and pinned up some of her sketches; some of them, many of them, are nudes, male and female. There are heads where she tried to paint eyes like mine. I think they are only sketches, very slight. She must have known somebody with eyes like mine. . . . I have pinned the most finished of the sketches so it sort of looks at me when I lie in bed.

Now it is I who am sending the blue airletters home. I half wish that Damion and I had not decided not to write. Sometimes I want to write to him, and to Sam the American, but, of course I never do—and never will.

You write such mundane things to your parents, Mr. Olson; I am writing such things in the journal I have to keep. It is my compulsion to—make everything that happens into words for an assignment and see it on your desk with "Excellent" written in the margin where you always put it. Do you find that sad? Just to want "Excellent" written in red pencil, Mr. Olson? Such a silly, small want . . .

Mike Tupp was flushed from unloading the oven. He leaned against the metal rack with its neatly piled rows of golden cooling loaves and he wiped his forehead on the blue-edged towel Angela tossed to him without standing up from the whitewood scrubbed table where she was taking her tea-break.

"Are they all like you back in Canada? Good lookers, I mean to say?" he asked with impertinence written all over his thin English face.

Angela crossed her eyes sickeningly and sucked her cheeks into horrible caves. It was all like a game in the bakehouse, a crazy game. She put her legs up on the white-painted chair next to her. Her legs ached on this last day of her first week's work.

"Now, now, I asked you a perfectly civil question. How about a civil answer, eh, Snowbird?"

She wrinkled her nose at him and rocked dangerously back on her chair. "Some bird! Yep. We're mass produced in the great North America. Thousands and thousands exactly like me."

"Wow-eee! I think I'll emigrate tomorrow." He tossed the towel back at her and she deftly caught it and reached over backwards to hang it on its hook by the sink, stretching without taking her feet down from the chair.

"Not much flesh on the bones though," he speculated eyeing her boldly, folding his arms and pursing his lips, managing to look lascivious and critical all at the same time.

"Keep your eyes for your own little sponge rolls, will ya, Mike Tupp," she gave him back a slice of English accent and the pert look she had picked up from Rita.

"This happens to be a free country, the mother of free countries, let me tell you, Miss America! Here a cat can look at a king, she can if she wants—and a king can spit back at a cat

92

—see! Don't eat much, do ya? Keep you short of food over there, eh?"

"We, young man," she mimicked some of the older customers who managed to buy yesterday's buns with queenly dignity, "we are raised on steaks, four-inch steaks, nothing less." She opened her eyes wide at him with film-starlet innocence. "No wonder English women get to look like foundered hippopotamuses. And it's a miracle to me that any of you have any teeth left after a lifetime of—all this." She waved her arm imperiously round the stacks of fancy cakes.

"Now now now, young woman, don't you go casting aspersions on our little tarts and our big cream horns," he said sternly and cocked an eyebrow at her.

"Ow, you are awful, Michael Tupp," Rita said bursting in the swing door from the shop with a large box on her hand. "I heard that. What ever is Ange going to think about us? Hey Ange, can you do this for me. There's two other people in and here's the Reverend wanting three dozen wet nellies to liven up his Ladies' Study Circle tonight. Can you reach them, duck? They've got pushed to the back." Rita giggled and paused before pushing back through the door. She admonished Mike as he walked over to help Angela reach the wet nellies for the Reverend's box. "Don't think my husband would let me work here if he knew what dirty-minded bastards I am forced to associate with. Don't you take no notice of him, Ange. Don't let him corrupt you!"

"Umph. Says she with a nasty wag of her delicious little butt. Don't hide much, her skirt, do it?" Mike sniffed and put one hand on Angela's behind as he handed forward wet nellies with the other.

"You're supposed to keep your eyes and your hands on the business, Mike me lad," Steve called across from washing his hands at the sink. "How the hell am I supposed to make me million with a wife globe-trotting and employees the like of what I've come up with?"

"Listen to the bloated bloody plutocrat, will ya. He can afford to send his missus off jet-setting off the slave labour of our poor proletarian fingers, then he dares stand there with his clean white hands and give us the heavy lip. How do you like that, eh? And I suppose you'd like me to get busy, work my fingers to the bone to trim up that bloody giant of a christening cake for the honourable Mrs. Starkey?"

Angela want back to sit down and finish her tea-break and watched Mike spreading out the decorations ready for the white icing job, little pink and silver cherubs and white daisies.

Steve flopped himself down on the chair at the other side of the table mopping at his big bald head with a big white handkerchief. "Tired, girl?" he asked. "Phew, the heat. Who'd want to run a bakery in the summer?"

Angela sipped her mug of tea and leaned back and smiled at him. Nice man. Big and jolly and kind. "Yea, I think I am kind of tired," she said. "I think I'll sleep in tomorrow. It's been such a lot of new things. Two weeks ago I was still at home with about three people per square mile."

"It's a wonder you're not suffering from culture shock, me girl," he said looking hard at her. "Yes, you get a good lie-in tomorrow. You're looking peaky. Thinner every day. Watch out, you'll break in two, kiddo."

She laughed and rinsed her cup at the tap, dried it on a tea-towel hooked on the wall, set the cup slowly back on the table, looked across at the work of art growing under the icing bag and Mike's clever fingers. "Pity the kid's not old enough to appreciate the fine job I'm doing on his behalf," he said and smiled, seeing her look across at him.

"Well, back to work," she said crossing her eyes at him again before she pushed through the swing doors into the shop, to the glare of the light from the big window with traffic roaring outside and faces, always faces peering in and pointing and choosing, and the till pinging, pinging, and Rita's constant chatter. Rita could talk all day and every day, cheerfully. Something bright to say to every customer. Angela was getting good at it too, copying the quick little witty inconsequentialities, the comments on the weather, and the inconsequential replies to inconsequential questions about her mother and her life in Canada. "Yes, it is very different, very different," she kept saying. "A lot more people. Yes, much hotter even in the shade. Yes, yes, my mother did do very well for herself, very well." Just like Grandmother had told everybody. But it was all tiring, hard on the legs as well as the mind. All the new names. Then the calculations in the strange money. She really had been too tired after work each day to do much more than ride around on her bike for a bit, then flop exhausted to sit on the little mat by the rough bookshelves and scribble in her exercise-book journal. Scribble, almost too tired to think, glad to die soon against the hot-water bottle and find death good.

"I could take you out, show you the sights of our city," Mike had proffered before she left on Saturday.

"Honest, I just want to sleep," she said. "Thanks all the same."

"The girl's right," Steve had joined in. "Leave her alone, Mike. She looks tired out."

"Are you sure you can put up with Old Mother Dawson?" Mike asked her knowingly. "She's not the most cheerful old lady to spend a weekend with."

Angela gave him a questioning look, wondering how he knew so much. "I've got my own room," she informed him. "Grandma means well. Can I take some old bread for the sparrows at my window, Steve?"

"Here," said Mike, "let me show you what my Mum does." He cut a length of string from the string roll, pushed a hole through half a dozen tough buns, threaded them on the string like a necklace. "Here," he said. "Hang this up outside your window and you'll get a real circus of sparrows to keep you happy."

"Aren't you the nice guy," she said fondly as she went out the back way to her bike in the bakery yard, stowing the bun necklace gratefully in the wicker basket.

"That's what all the girls say," he called after her and stood in the doorway watching her go. "You should get to know me better, Snowbird."

She cycled away, laughing. The first week had ended and her wages were in her bag, the first wages to save for whatever was to come. But she was so tired.

Her dinner warming between two plates smelled like liver and onions and Grandpa had met her at the gate to tell her Grandma was down the road visiting and she was to look after herself. Obsessed by the moment of good fortune, her mind worked frantically over the possible ways of disposing of the dinner. Too lumpy to wash down the sink, too dangerous to carry the plates to a toilet. She remembered seeing paper bags among the socks and tangled nylons under the cushion on the couch. She scraped the brown supper into a brown paper bag over the sink and rushed out with it to the flush toilet down the yard, hiding it all the way behind her shoulder bag. Then she washed the dishes and put them away, jubilant at her good fortune, released into daring and creativity. While Grandma was out she would sweep off the crumbs and put them on the window ledge outside the living-room window. The window wouldn't open so she had to walk outside and up the yard to shake the crumbs off the sheet of newspaper. There had been a letter from home on the table propped up against the milk bottle. She saved it to read in her bedroom, the first letter from home.

But first she opened her window wide and hung the bread necklace from the window catch, left it swinging in the open window.

She lay on the bed to read the pages, three pages in her mother's neat, plain handwriting. Such a lot had happened at home, she read, and her mother had not written sooner because she had been in such a whirl. It appeared that Damion's father had something to do with a farm exhibit at the Calgary Stampede and that by chance Damion had told some official there about the Moynahan wall hangings. "This year there is a large arts and crafts section, very exciting, as part of the Stampede." Anyhow, the outcome was that Damion's father had brought somebody out to see the wall hangings and five of them were being exhibited. "Would you believe, I keep being referred to as A Canadian Artist!!!!!" Dinah put in the five exclamation marks. Angela felt an excitement under her mother's words. She had never had a letter from her mother before. Perhaps Sam the American was right. And dear, dear Damion! Other news; her father was very tired, said he missed her. Gordon was doing a lot of the work. Gordon sent his love.

Angela lay back and watched the sparrows chirping and bringing their friends to swing and peck on the necklace. She was tired. The room was chill. She crept into bed with her clothes on and slept before Grandmother brought the hot-water bottle.

Time began to move slowly and a loneliness slipped into the monotony of the weeks. One Sunday morning, somebody somewhere in the house made coffee and Angela woke to the faint scent of the prairie kitchen, her mother turning the bacon in the bright orange, wide, generous skillet, and she was overwhelmed with homesickness. She lay watching the sparrows chirping and cheeping on another necklace of buns and a sunbeam, small thing, skittered across her ceiling, but she didn't want to get up, face going down into the house, alien food and alien smells of old men in bathrooms, the difficulties of washing her hair, or getting a bath in the cold bathroom. She rebuked herself. Couldn't she remember when she had to wash her hair in a bowl on the yellow kitchen table with her father grumbling? And her brother, Rory, had never lived with a bathroom at all. She knew she had grown soft but she winced at the tensions she felt in the house. Culture shock, Mr. Olson. The streets are familiar, and the way the people talk, I found a park and a band in the park and I have sat and watched the world of England walk by. But English days all end up chilly and I ride home and dread going into the house. But the grandparents are kind . . . will the two months never go?

She weakened against her best intentions. She agreed to go out with Mike Tupp all day on the last Sunday in July. He said, "Come on, Snowbird, let Uncle Mike put some roses in your cheeks and show you the countryside."

Rita put in her twopenny-worth of persuasion and offered to lend Angela her crash helmet and leather jacket because she wasn't going nowhere till that husband of hers had painted the front room. Even Steve had encouraged her to get out and meet some young people and see a bit more of the country while it was summer. A nice bunch of kids the motorcycle club that Mike rode with.

Grandma had reacted sourly, turning down her mouth and looking at her suspiciously. "There and I thought what a sensible girl you were leaving the men alone. I thought you were one of them with their heads screwed on the right way. Just see and behave yourself. Let me just warn you that you're better off in this world without men around." The remarks had slipped into whines. "If I had my time over there'd be no man messing up my life, I'm telling you." She had the cunning look of Madeleine about her as bitterness and sour wisdom hung about her words. Angela felt embarrassed for her grandfather who sat and smiled his rheumy smile and dragged on his cigarette, moving his eyes through the smoke lovingly from one to the other of the women.

"You take no notice of your grandma," he said softly at last. "It's all talk. She doesn't mean a word of it, not my old dutch. You have a good time while you can, me love."

And it was a good time, exhilarating to ride behind Mike on a motorbike, one more in the roar of twenty powerful machines, scaring the highways and rousing the narrow country roads. While the engines were roaring she felt like a member of the tribe and she shouted with them, clung onto Mike, and sang with them, shouting into the wind. She bounced up and down on the seat and prayed that there would somewhere be a bump hard enough to loosen her insides. Motorbiking appealed. It was reckless. But when they pulled up at a little country pub for lunch and filled up the tables on the outside lawn, and Mike kept putting his arm about her and making a show of her being his girl, in the wisecracks and banter and dirty jokes and girls giggling and screaming, she was Angela-on-the-outside again, right back where she had always been, that super-clever girl with nothing to say. She flung crumbs to the pigeons that waddled around on the soft of the green green grass and she listened to the froth subsiding on the great mugs of beer and she watched herself in the film she was making on track seven of the videotape of her mind and she called it *Captive Sunday*, like a title, a sequence, a small chapter.

She was glad when the machines were taking them again farther into the scent of summer, fields and woodlands. She looked round Mike at the long road ahead and wished they could ride on and on and on forever. But they stopped at an old castle, parked the bikes and spread a picnic in the shade of a crumbling wall, and like kids, in between bursts of refreshment they climbed and yelled and squealed over the mellow yellow stone walls, saying "Boo!" to each other through sudden hidden windows, balancing recklessly on uneven narrow walls. Then when the mood died they broke up in pairs and headed for the woods. Mike took her hand and told her he knew where there was a super lake, if she felt like walking.

She felt like walking and it was cool and lush and fragrant with damp grasses and loud with bird song through the quiet of the old trees.

"Makes you feel romantic," Mike whispered, squeezing her hand and pulling her closer to him.

She said nothing, listened to the green silence.

"Bet your mother remembers this place. It's covered with bluebells, a sea of bluebells in springtime. All the kids bike out here from miles away when the bluebells are out."

"We don't have bluebells where I grew up," she said and it sounded lame. She wished she weren't here with Mike. She didn't feel romantic and she found herself walking quicker and frowning. Then the ground marshed down to a pretty lake edged with rushes and trees hanging over. He breathed an ecstatic sigh and pulled her closer. She was aware of his fingers spread across her ribs. "Bet you don't have nothing like this in Canada," he whispered and nuzzled her ear.

"Nothing so sugar sweet," she fended him off. "There's a lake in dry desert near to my home. No trees. A white edge of dry scum. But it's much bigger than this. Whose are the boats?" she said, pointing to two green punts tethered to bent overhanging trees.

"Some fisherman's," he said, diverted, the adventurer rising in his eyes. "Let's take a sail, eh? Come on." And he was pulling her round the lakeside to the nearest bobbing boat. He was quick to pick up a long broken branch for a pole, untie the rope, get her seated and push off, Columbus in the tilt of the nose and the flash of the dark eyes. He laughed delightedly and gave the little boat a good push off while he stood up across it, a minor Colossus. She looked through the span of his long tight jeans and laughed. Then it was too deep for his pole to touch bottom and he nearly fell over. She laughed out loud and he swore and their voices echoed and re-echoed prettily from afar.

"Hey, we're sinking," she said and pointed to the water rising above the well boards up into the boat. He tried to push hard again but leaned drastically, then lost his pole. "Perhaps you should sit down," she giggled and tried to bail out some of the water with her cupped hands.

"Can you swim?" he asked her, still looking down from his height.

"Yea."

"Wish I could. It's deep, ain't it?"

She heard a bit of pathos in his voice and looked up at him with concern. "Sit down, Mike," she said quietly. "Honest, if you can't swim, sit down. That's it. Gently." When he was safely seated she added, "My brother was drowned in a boating accident—and he could swim."

"Job's bloody comforter, aren't you kid?'

"Help me bail," she said and saw sweat beading on his eyebrows and over his top lip. "Actually I don't think we're going to take in any more. We've reached equilibrium."

"Good job we're both thin, eh?" He leaned back and looked around, playing at being all easy again. "Now for speed," he shouted. "Full speed ahead for the far shore. All oars to the wheel," and he started paddling with his hands strongly; she made her hands do the same and the little punt moved through the still water across the middle of the lake. He started to sing loudly, "Sixteen men on the dead man's chest, yo-ho-ho and a bottle of rum," and his voice came back in a confusion of echoes. Eventually they reached shore, sliding through the floating leaves of waterlilies, then shushed the boat onto the soft muddy bottom. "Whew," he said. "That calls for a rest." They walked a few steps from the lake edge and he flopped down under a spread tree. She sat down by him with her arms round her knees, looking out past a yellow lily across the green water, past the soft foam of the trees to the silver of the English sky. He reached out and pulled her down by the shoulder and the grasses were above their heads and big orange and brown butterflies flew over their eyes, and the silence moved in under the birdsongs, into the grass-scented sunshine skittering through the leaves.

For a while they lay as though drinking in the peace, following their own thoughts, till he interrupted to ask abruptly. "Hey.
Are you on the pill?"

"Me?" she responded foolishly.

"No me, you dope. You do have the pill in Canada, don't
you?"

"What's it to you?" she asked turning away and watching a
daddy-longlegs tread leg by leg through the forest of the grasses.

"Oh come on, Angie. You didn't think we were going to
waste all this, did ya?"

She watched the daddy-longlegs reach up to the sky of his
day. A ladybug settled on a grass near her nose. She blew on
him. "I'm not wasting anything," she said, and added the
cloud that passed over the sun to the track seven videotape in
her mind, and tonight she'd remember it in her journal. She
felt her skin go goose-pimply.

"Oh come on, Angie. Don't try to make out you don't fancy
me."

She turned to him and opened her eyes wide and laughed in
real and mock outrage. "Well," she expostulated, and half sat
up. "You cheeky thing, you." Isn't that what Rita would say,
in an accent just like that too. "Well, Michael Tupp! The very
cheek of you to imagine that I'm waiting here just lusting for
your bod. Well. Well. Well."

He made a grab for her and pushed her down into the grasses
again and crushed a violent, meant-to-be-virile kiss, that went
crooked, on her lips, and his teeth pushed through to kill the
romance. She struggled against him but laughed behind her
closed mouth in shudders that rocked her. Then he pushed his
hands under her smock and made contact with her body flesh
deftly, as one with much practice. He pushed her bra up over
her breasts and for a moment she leaned into him wondering
whether to respond. His hands were warm and friendly. If she
let him do it hard maybe it would jolt her insides. She kissed
him and felt his hand on her belly, undoing her jeans zipper,
his hand exploring the curve of her belly, fingering down inside
her panties—then she closed her eyes and—he was Gordon
Kopec. Her mind went cold. She pulled up her knee and felled
him.

101

He was up and on his feet holding his hurt with both hands cupped, doubled up, and dancing to his groans. She laughed harshly and looked at him with ice, calmly wriggled herself down into her bra. She picked up her shoulder bag and swung it round and round her head, "Come again, Romeo, and I'll bash your brains in. I ain't a farm-girl for nothing," she pointed and mocked at his discomfiture.

He laughed too, good-naturedly. "You're a rotten little bugger, aren't you? Nobody's Angel, you! And don't tell me you couldn't take a fancy to me—I know about these things." He laughed at himself and stood holding his hurt in both hands, still wincing and grouching.

"Sorry about that, Mike," she turned kind sensing she ought to rebuild his ego. "Nothing personal, honest." Now she felt like a mother punishing and wheedling a naughty boy.

"Don't you worry, Snowbird. I'll get you yet. That's a promise," he said knowingly, with his pert expression restored and an eyebrow cocked, and she laughed because it wasn't important, just *Captive Sunday*, track seven.

They rolled up their pants and waded through the mud to the green boat that had slipped away while they weren't looking. They giggled and laughed as they climbed into it, then grew silent and pensive as they slowly paddled back, hardly disturbing the green sheen of the water. When he caught her eye he put on a mild mocking expression as though she had failed in something and he was the gentle wise man.

It was like that back at work. He came up behind her time and again during the day, put his hands on her waist, touched her behind or her cheek and whispered sweet nothings just for her—as though she needed encouragement.

He teased her for her purity to entertain Rita and Steve. "Can't get anywhere with her," he'd say, or words to that effect, and Rita would always say, "Oh Mike, you are awful," and once Steve said in warning, "You want to watch out for these Englishmen, Angie me duck. They never know when they're beat. They never give up."

Angela laughed, fooled around harder, sharpened her tongue to the bakeshop ways, and behind the banter, the fun, the funny faces she made, she wrangled in the increasing madhouse of her mind. Six cream horns, set them side by side in a tissue-smooth box; our Dinah brought home flowers; did well for herself in Canada; leave the men alone, no good comes of them; are you all right?; old men stink up the bathrooms; that funny little look; are you all right eh? duck?; Gordon sends his love.

The letters from home were rare. Short. Rushed, happy notes because Dinah was busy. Somebody actually was prepared to pay for her work and she had been commissioned to make an extra-large hanging depicting Prairie Harvest. Joe Moynahan was not well but he sent his love, twice wrote a couple of lines at the bottom of the page telling her to look after her money, be careful on that bicycle and stay clear of getting mixed up with trash. Then he put four kisses and signed "Your ever loving Dad". Gordon always sent his love.

Mike Tupp began walking her home from the bakery, pushing her bike with one hand and holding her hand in the other, then they would lean against the wall where the tree reached over and gently continue the teasing of the day, each for a separate reason putting off the moment when she pushed her bike through door 107.

She kept reminding him he was wasting his time because she would be gone in a month, in three weeks, in two weeks. He would wind a strand of her hair round his finger, round his wrist, and tug her slowly to him and tell her she wasn't going to get away, that he had other intentions. Then she would cross her eyes, or tread on his toe when he was nearest being romantic.

Twice more she went out with the motorbike club, clinging onto him for crazy, spinning, noisy, wind-crashing miles, and she clowned the private time away playing him for fun-loving kid, not great lover, and some evenings they sat in the park on a green slatted bench and made remarks about everybody who walked by, naughty remarks, cheeky words, funny for a crazy moment, and she held his hand gratefully because he made her not alone, and she counted the weeks to leaving, the days, because it was getting too hard to stay.

The dress she had worn on the plane, slight as a morning shadow, she could no longer wear. She stood in front of the mahogany wardrobe mirror sideways-on and she tried to draw the bulge in, in to what had once been the concavity of her stomach. She tugged the gentle dress to try and smooth the tight wrinkles away from her hips. If she held her breath and pulled her stomach in hard—the dress might pass—but it was not possible to hold in so long. She hated herself. Bulging thing. She drooped, let her breasts hang low and her belly sag forward, deliberately sagged herself out so the dress clung and wrinkled till she looked like a back-street woman pregnant with tired despairs. And she looked, sickened, into the tragedy of her own eyes, then put her tongue out at her own silly face, dragged herself out of the dress and hid it in the shoe compartment of her flight bag. Lots of women live with that much stick-out, anyhow. Nobody could really tell. Nobody was going to tell.

On the Tuesday of the second week in August she made an excuse to leave work early, thus not having Mike walk her home, and she cycled across town, through the heavy traffic, to the anonymity of a large department store and bought three strong beige panty-girdles. She chose the ones that looked to her like suits of armour and had satin reinforced fronts guaranteed to hold in sags and bulges, like the ones she'd laughed at in the catalogue at home.

Before she left the store, she disposed of the lingerie bag, all the wrappings, pushed the girdles under all her junk down at the bottom of her peacock bag, wanting no strange evidence for her grandmother's eyes or tell-tale things to confirm Madeleine's shrewd yellow certainty.

Next morning she turned the key in her bedroom door and tugged and twisted herself into the unfamiliar elasticated tight constriction of a girdle. She hid the other two under the rolled-up dress in the shoe part of her flight bag and now she stood like a model from Eaton's catalogue, posing in bra and girdle; but not quite like a model, because her ribs were too definitely making corrugated patterns through her skin and her arms looked pathetic just above the elbows. Still, the girdle seemed to do the trick and she breathed relief. She was flat again and not enough flesh to bulge above it to show prying eyes what she was wearing. She began the day feeling firm and comfortably held together, newly encouraged that she could maintain her secret for sure now for the two remaining weeks.

But it was not that easy. As the day grew hotter and longer so the girdle cut in tighter. Whenever she could, when nobody was looking she bent behind the counter and eased its elastic cut out of one groin, then the other. It curled up round the waist edge, folded over and cut into her, cruel as wet leather, so she had difficulty not being irritable even with the customers. When Mike walked her home she was torn between whether to linger in the alley uncomfortable with him, wriggling her weight from leg to leg trying to ease the nick of the elastic legs between her thighs, or rush in out of the hot afternoon into the hotter house that would be smelling of her hot dinner.

"Touchy, aren't you?" Mike humoured her putting his hands on the black wall behind her shoulders and swaying back and forth above her.

"It's so hot," she said and moved from one hip to the other against the wall, then back again.

"Eh, keep doing that," he said, "it's right sexy."

She wanted to scream, to kick him, and she looked at him with maddened eyes. "Then I'd better go in right now," and she pushed against his confining arm. "Wouldn't do to get sexy here in the alley with all these windows watching."

He held his arms steady, holding her in. She tried to duck under. But he stopped her.

"Say please to Uncle Mike," he teased and she wanted to scream. She pushed against his arm again to no avail, and with horror felt herself crumple into weeping, and rushed her hands to hide her face.

"Hey Angie," he said and tried to pull her hands away, gently. "Hey, Angie, what's up?"

She leaned against him, then drew away. "It's so hot," she said and sighed, trying not to fight against the cutting in between her thighs. "The humidity gets at people from the prairies," she tried to tell him and said she'd better go in before she fainted or something.

Inside the dinner smell Grandmother was whining and waving three airletters. "She can't find time to write to us but here are two for you from our Dinah. Maybe there's something gone wrong. Two letters. And they're both posted the same day," she said, peering at the postmarks with them close up to her glasses.

Angela's insides felt suddenly empty and the whole of her body telescoped down into the pain of cutting elastic between her thighs. Her father! Something had happened to her father. In every letter there had been something to say he was—not right.

"And there's this other one." Grandmother was holding the third airletter up to her glasses. Don't know who this is from. Somebody named Good. Posted the day after."

"Thanks," was all she said as she snatched the three from the old lady's hand and rushed past her upstairs to her room to tug and pull the girdle off her body to rest crumpled round her knees—oh blessed relief—while she lay back on the bed to open first the one from Damion. Her heart pounded. Why would he write unless something dreadful had happened? Her fingers couldn't unseal the glue. She rummaged in her bag to find a nail file to slit the airletter open. Bold writing done easy with a felt-tip. But short. A note. She had forgotten. "Congratulations. My dear Chinese pussycat, I can just see you smiling now. You beat me. So what's new, Pussycat. You got the highest marks in the province." He said he would be flying up north the first week in September and would probably be back about May. And he missed her. Too bad about Mr. Olson, wasn't it?

She put the blue airletter, with its pale goose flying, against her cheek and through an unwanted brim of tears watched a sparrow hovering over the nibbled and broken remains of yesterday's bread necklace.

Mr. Olson? What was too bad about Mr. Olson?

The second letter from her mother was only written because

the first had already been sealed when Gordon brought in the mail with the examination results in it. . . . Dinah told how the rest of the grade twelves had done and that Damion had got very high marks and qualified for a scholarship. Gordon sent his congratulations too. A parcel had been in the mail for her from Mr. Olson with instructions to forward it. She would send it c/o Canada House because Angela would be on her travels by the time it came by slow mail, and it would be best for her to pick it up as she passed through London.

The first letter said that summer was still cold and wet and that her father seemed tired; there was talk of a road being paved through to Calgary. She was still working on the harvest wall hanging and was getting all sorts of attention from all over the place for her work. Gordon sent his love. Her father had written on the bottom in pencil, "I am giving Ami a handful of oats for you. Your ever loving Dad." And four kisses.

So she had got the scholarship.

Against every instinct to leave it off and flop, she pulled the girdle back up from round her knees and tried to smooth out its folded places so they cut less. She went down to placate her grandmother and pay her respects to the saved dinner. She took her mother's letters to read bits of them to Grandma.

"Well?" Grandma whined. "What was all that about that you had to go upstairs to read it?"

"I had to go to the bathroom," Angela lied to calm the old lady. "The extra letter was just to tell me my examination results. I got a scholarship," she added, trying to make the atmosphere friendlier.

"Well, I only hope it does you more good than our Dinah's ever did her, that's all I hope." She went and brought in the meal and Angela noticed that the tea was already made. "Nice bit of fresh young rabbit," Grandma gloated as she took off the top plate and opened the swimming meal. "Our Dinah got a big scholarship to art school, in London. One of the biggest scholarships in England and gave it all up for that man. Come on now, eat up. Don't look at it like that."

The girdle cut in again like a string tightening round her waist, anguish round her thighs. She couldn't stand the smell of the meat and the swim of gravy.

107

"Lovely fresh young rabbit. Saved you a nice juicy leg. Come on, pick it up in your fingers. Come on, me duck, our Dinah's going to take one look at you and think we never treated you to a square meal."

The girdle contracted, squeezed, tied itself in knots of pain. She couldn't touch the flesh of that rabbit. What could she do? She frowned to contain the pity she had to feel for her poor old grandmother who had put forth her best, was pleading for it, and was going to have it cast off, rejected, hated, treated like nothing, hurt worse than the knives of the girdle.

"Grandma." She bit her lip and tried to smile with a believable expression, like murder without hurt. "Grandma. I don't feel good. I don't think I can eat anything." She held her grandma in the cradle of a smile and the old woman wheeled her child. "Oh come on now, me duck. Try just a little bit. Just a tiny bit. It'll make you feel better to get a bit of something good inside you." She took a fork and the butter knife and broke open the flesh for Angela to see how good it was.

The girl felt her stomach rising. She stood up too quickly from the wound in the rabbit flesh, knocked her chair back clumsily. "Oh Grandma," she pleaded, trying to hold on to her kindness. "Grandma, I'm sorry. I can't," and before the words were finished she knew she'd done her murder.

The old woman's poor face went blank, then the wrinkles reformed in all the patterns of past uglinesses and Angela sat down again to face the face that was a wizened thing of horror and despair, maddened out of every tender line.

"Not good enough for you, is it? I can see you finding fault. I wasn't born yesterday. Not good enough for you. I can tell by the look on your face what you're thinking." Angela sat up, pulling herself in inside the pressures of the girdle and tried to turn off while the tirade lasted. Please God, don't let me answer. Please God. Her turned-off eyes looked into her grandmother's faded madness sprinkling hate behind the rimless glasses. "Like your mother. I know that insolent look from her days. We were never good enough for her once she got her education. Not good enough, we weren't. Ingratitude. That's all parents earn for all their sacrifices. Ingratitude! If I had my time over, I can tell you there'd be no children nor grandchildren round this house to mock us with their ingratitude. Children! They bring you nothing but trouble and grief. The country takes your boys and you're not good enough for the girls."

Would she never stop? The girdle was like fire in her groins and she eased herself from buttock to buttock till the movement came like rocking to the hypnotic anger of the words coming out of the wrinkled mouth from between the porcelain evenness of china-white, spittle-shiny teeth.

"Like your mother. Just like your mother. We're not good enough for you. She could afford to come home every year, if she wanted to. She never did care about us." The voice is shouting now, wild uncontrolled invective. Angela breathes slowly to keep control, keep sane in the lashing words. She steadies her hands and puts the top plate back over the mess of the dinner, and she leans forward with her hands both still on the warm plate and her eyes very wide and bland, a wall against the raving.

"She never cared about us. Left us she did the first chance that came her way. Left us for a dirty old man old enough to be her father. Filthy old bugger. Filthy rotten sod doing that to my Dinah. My Dinah, nothing but a girl, my lovely girl!" She was screaming.

"Stop it!" The shout that broke loose was full-throated, enormous, a blast to break through walls. "Stop it. You cruel old woman!" She struggled to shout louder. "Stop it. Stop it." And she heard her own shouts and watched her own break-down. "Stop it. Stop it. Stop it." This must be what a nervous breakdown is, while the sane you stands back mesmerized watching a game called madness. "Stop it," she thundered as though to complete the exercise of her own amazement at her own violence. She took her hands away from the plates where they had sat so still like strangers sane on the edge of the carnage and she stood up deliberately, aloof from herself, stood behind the chair dismayed that she had lost control. She looked at her grandmother's wrinkled fingers clawing against the chest of the colourless woollen cardigan that hung like a dirty shroud from the brittle thin shoulders, and she wished the shouting had never exploded. How could she ever undo it now? The harm? She felt chilled, sick inside, defeated by her own weakness. It was there forever.

But Grandmother was a mouth again, a mouth working in stretched spittle and wrinkles, and the cheeks round the mouth were wet from the eyes that were cold as a lizard's. "Like mother like daughter! We have you here out of the goodness of our hearts, living off us, off us two poor old people, and do you show us any gratitude? No. No. There's no gratitude in you. Turn your nose up at us. Shouting at your old grandmother like that. You should be ashamed." She was crying now and whining. Angela stood with her hands on the chair-back not knowing what to do, crossing her legs on the agony between her thighs. "Shouting at me! Your own grandmother, who has loved you and tried to do my best for you. After I've lived to slave my fingers to the bone to educate two children above their station. What have I ever got out of it but heartbreak? One to spill his blood for his country. My only daughter to prostitute herself to an old man. What have I ever got out of it, I should like to know. Now an ungrateful granddaughter sponging off us, taking all she can get out of us. Old people like us."

"Well, we can soon change that." It came out too loud. She felt silly. Her grandfather had come in from the yard without a cigarette and he stood with a drained face looking at them from the doorway. "I can leave, right now, if you like," she ended quietly.

Grandfather looked more bent and worn than ever. "Now, now, you two. I could hear you down at the bottom of the yard." He bent his way past Angela across to stand by his wife and he put his arms round her shoulders. "You don't have to take any notice of your grandmother, Angela, me duck. She just gets excited. She doesn't mean a word of it." He stroked the old lady's hair and held her protectively to him, spoke wheedlingly. "It's just her way, me duck. Always was. She gets carried away. Don't mean a word of it."

By now Grandma was crying and sobbing out loud, mopping her cheeks with the backs of both hands like a child, tears flooding from under her glasses.

What to do?

110

She looked at her brown hands so calm on the chair-back. Her hands. Foreign calm. She sighed. It was hopeless!

"I'm sorry, Grandpa," she said. "Sorry, Grandma. I shouldn't have lost my temper. I'm sorry. I'll go out on my bike, ride the crotchety out, if you don't mind," and without looking for their reaction she walked out through the rabbit stew of the kitchen and the gravy-thick savoury of the scullery, out into the yard with the hot sun trapped in its walls, stifling.

She rushed her bicycle out into the walled alley and stood on one pedal to bump freewheeling, jolt, jolt, jolt, down the crazed length of the cobblestoned fortress moat of houses' back entrances.

She had left her blue, gooseflying airletters in the crumbs by the milkbottle on the table, Damion in crumbs, four scrawled kisses by the butter dish, a scholarship, her mother's excitement —but they were another world. Prairies away.

Left behind.

Now she was out of the house and the violence of the tension, her fingers quivered on the handlebars and she was trembling quite apart from the shuddering set up through the bike and herself by the rude irregularities of the back alley's big old cobblestones. Although neither the jolts nor the trembling seemed likely to dislodge her insides cramped in the tight security of the oppressive girdle! She coasted on one pedal, not avoiding the worst of the jutting slabs. She watched the front tire turning, willingly mesmerized, pensive about nothing, inert in her trajectory, until the back wheel hissed out of its buoyancy, bumped, flobbed; it was flat. She stood down and her shoulders sagged as she looked back at the flattened rubber. This is not my day, she thought, and accepted hopelessness as she propped the bike up against the nearest wall and with unskilled fingers set about pumping up the tire the way she had seen her father, her grandfather do it. She pumped awkwardly, the wheel slipping against her efforts and the tire barely inflating, while her mind flinched irritably round the edges of her girdle.

"I'm afraid it's not going to work," a crisp female voice said dryly behind her, arresting her so that she half turned round with her hands still on the pump, seeing first bare feet on a wet step, then a tall, severe, white-haired elderly woman with a garden hose in her hands by the green doorway into backyard 252.

"Good Lord!" the woman said sharply and turned the nozzle to stop the flow of water. "Good Lord," she said again, frowning down at the girl whose startled eyes registered surprise, then panic, then frowned and hung tangled with the intense white gaze of the older woman. For the moment of impact Angela was puzzled by the familiarity of the look. Her frown deepened as she straightened up slowly to face the face with her own eyes looking back from another age, the eyes she had seen in her

112

mother's sketches, frighteningly fierce. Her hands shook and she gripped the pump viciously and bit hard into her lip to stop its quivering. So! My Scandinavian ancestor!

"Forgive me," the woman said and eased her gaze. "It's just that I seem to be seeing ghosts. There used to be a girl, lived up the street," she raised her arm and pointed up the alley, a positive gesture from a tall spare woman, "years ago. Silly of me. I suddenly felt that you were she." She laughed, deep throated. "Old age plays funny tricks with our sense of time. That girl would be almost a middle-aged woman by now."

"My mother. Dinah Dawson," Angela said shortly and turned away to the bike again because the woman said, "Good Lord," twice again like an unthinkable revelation and the pale eyes probed her, her the ghost, and she saw the rabbit leg with the butter knife opening its flesh in the brown gravy, and she wanted to avoid looking, but the woman wouldn't let her; she was possessive.

"Look," she said briskly, "there's somebody in here who will fix your bike if you want to bring it in," the tone of voice not offering any choice. But she didn't have any choice, did she? She considered, wavered, then unscrewed the pump from the wheel. The woman was calling back into the yard, "Fred, Fred dear, you can mend a puncture for this young woman, can't you?" There was authority in her and she held the gate while Angela lifted the bike over the wet steps, then paused—arrested—halfway through, like Damion Good on the threshold of her mother's kitchen. But she caught herself, held aloof from comment, walked nonchalantly into the surprise of rioting colour towards a dark young man who was coming towards her with a small boy holding onto his hand across the wet shine of the yard's black tiles to take the bike from her. He lifted it and turned it round carefully between the tubs of freshly watered marigolds and nasturtiums. The air was pungent. Like being in a summer greenhouse. So this must be the yard with the other tree, the edge of which she could see when she sat on her grandparents' wall. But this tree grew not at the end of the yard, by the wall, as did the one in the Dawson yard, but out of the middle of the foot of the L, and the tiles had been uprooted and replaced by a small circle of brown earth, oasis in the black.

113

Under the spread of the tree's shade three striped canvas chairs shouted of summer. The walls round the yard, to a full height of seven feet, had all been painted with a warm pink-earth colour that was now splattered with patterns of brown where the watering had freshly shadowed it. Fred said not to worry about her bike, he'd have it ready in no time, and the woman said to sit under the tree and—she didn't finish.

"Wait a minute, we need a drink," she said and went away to go into the house by the far door where Fred was upturning the bike with the child watching; a trim woman, watched from behind, young when the lines of the face weren't seen to define the years, a trim body in a pale tailored dress, her bare legs and feet still young, striding easily, her hair straight white and pulled severely into a knot on top of her head. So! Angela breathed out the tremors of quakes like a child who has cried for too long. She opened her mouth to fill her lungs with the full violence of the scent of drenched marigolds. If she closed her eyes her grandmother's voice was a mouth again screaming, "filthy rotten old sod, doing that to my Dinah." My Dinah. My Dinah. My Mother. Oh My Mother. What did she do? She shuddered and shook her head not knowing where to put her aching mind. She leaned back into the give of the canvas chair and looked up through the leaves into the green heart of the tree, sanity in there holding still, and she wriggled herself to make the sit of the girdle bearable. She touched the spider dangling near her hair, flicked it so it wound itself back up its thread back to the dusty old web stretched precarious between two branches.

"I have your mother to thank for this tree, your mother and my son." She was brisk, talked without sentiment. "It's an offshoot from the one up at Dawson's. I suppose you are staying with your grandparents?" She talked as she sat down, unscrewing a black stopper from a bulbous green bottle, then pouring the contents, golden, spitting bubbles, into two tall glasses, using the floor for a table. "Cider?" she asked and put a cold brimming glass into Angela's hand. "What did they call you, by the way? I'm Clara. Clara Jonason."

"Angela. Angela Moynahan." She sipped at the bitter-sweet apple taste and felt the bubbles breaking in fragments

114

against her nose. "I've never had cider before," she said for something unimportant to say to fend off the thing they might say, and she looked up into the eyes of the other who was observing her too intensely, threatening her composure. "You must be the mother of the boy in Grandmother's photographs, the blond boy," she said, ventured, and pressed her ankles together because she was trembling.

Clara nodded and looked at her quizzically, holding the green-tinted glass to the deep lines in her cheek, then smiling a slow rich smile so the other pale eyes had to smile back. "Hardly a boy any more." She laughed the throaty laugh again. "He is the same age as Dinah. They pretty well grew up together, you know. Did you know? Did Dinah tell you?" Angela looked away and frowned. "Just Grandma showed me the photos," she said flatly and drank hard to empty the glass of its cider, making the swallowing roar in her ears so she wouldn't have to listen to what Clara Jonason was thinking. Why hadn't her mother told her? Her Mother!

Clara stretched her long legs and looked down at her bare feet, drew lines with her toe on the drying tiles from a remaining puddle of water. "It doesn't seem so long ago to me, strange as it may seem to you. Dinah half lived here. She and Jeff started school together, got their scholarships together—although Dinah was the cleverer one. This tree was one of their escapades." She went on to tell how they had climbed too far along a branch of the Dawson tree and been terrified out of their wits by the multiplicity of disasters when it broke off, tearing a scar on the mother tree, rending Dinah's best knickers, skinning one side of Jeff's face and both knees. She had arrived home from work to find two filthy miserable sinners and a hell of a mess of a hole in the middle of the yard. "We planted the poor broken branch. Twenty-six summers ago." The laugh again. "It wasn't much of a tree when Dinah left, nothing like this." The laugh again.

What was there to laugh about? Angela laughed too, the same deep laugh, because the cider was beginning to make her mind feel vague at the edges and the trembling had subsided. She leaned back watching the woman through her eyelashes, watching the woman trying to reach her, but underneath the warm cider drowsiness great surges of tenderness and compassion kept rising up, almost to make tears for her father, her poor father, poor old, kind old Joe Moynahan. He had been so good to her.

"My mother still plants trees." She told the facts of making wind-breaks on the prairie.

"We never heard from Dinah after she left for her summer in Canada. She was so excited about going. But she just disappeared from our lives." Clara's voice went on evenly but her eyes searched for explanation.

"She met my Dad." She said it gently as though it were true, a warm thing. She said it from under her eyelashes and watched the quick look of inquiry. "The very first week. The neighbours all say it was a wild and lightning love affair," she let the cider let her laugh in her throat like the other woman who raised her eyebrows and laughed too.

The bike was fixed and propped against the pink wall by the gate but Angela stayed because she had no will to leave, because the woman wanted her there. The cider, the warm evening trapped in the summer-filled yard was healing. Besides she didn't want to face the moment of going back up the alley to her grandparents, her grandmother's tongue.

Clara said wasn't it a coincidence, "the first day I've been home in two months and you get a puncture right outside my gate. I leave again on Saturday, but you must come and have dinner with me on Friday." She explained that she still chose to work, she loved it. She was a private nurse at present working with a very interesting case in a village fifty miles away.

Answering questions about her mother's art, Angela lied, and she didn't know why. "Oh yes, she kept it up. She just had an exhibition in Calgary," she said and it sounded so splendid, so successful. She almost got her peacock shoulder bag from the basket on the handlebars of the bike, but changed her mind. Maybe it wasn't much; anyhow it was grubby now.

"What happened to your son?" she asked and pretended to be intent on removing a fat green caterpillar from the back of a nasturtium leaf it was chewing into lace.

"He's a pretty successful musician. Violinist."

116

"No, I mean him, his private life," she said and wound the caterpillar round her finger, watching its yellow feet.

Clara frowned a moment and sucked her cheeks in, and Angela listened to her trying to be honest. "I think I have said it all if I say he is a distinguished musician. I think his private life is incidental. He has had two brief marriages. No children. You should visit him, in London," she said as she drained the last of the cider into the glasses. "I'll be there for the first two weeks in September, taking a holiday. I'll give you his address and phone number. We could have dinner together, all of us. If you're still in England."

She unwound the caterpillar and set it back on a strong leaf. "If I'm still in England," she said and laughed. Two more weeks. The girdle would be too tight. It was pressing in again.

"Your father? When we heard Dinah had married, we thought he must have been—very special, to keep her from coming back to take up the scholarship in London. She had worked so hard for that." Clara held Angela's gaze and Angela thrust up her chin.

"He still is very special," she said, and felt tears at the injustice, guilt because she hadn't loved him for so long, terrible compassion because his son, his child had been drowned. "A wild and generous fiddle-playing Irishman. A very kind man," she said. "You should just see the community hall he designed and helped build; it's a work of art," she said, and let waves of cider and sentiment wash through her, the more powerful, she realized, because she hadn't eaten since her slice of dry toast at breakfast. And when they decided to go in out of the falling cool she had to remind herself to walk carefully, keep a hold on the sway of her senses, and was glad when Clara brought out bread and cheese which they ate sitting on the rug by a small fire with the street lights shining in through the big bay window of the front room, in the house that was identical to the Dawsons' in structure, but in atmosphere a galaxy away. This was bright and pastel-shaded where the Dawsons' was brown and dark. Clara occupied the whole of the long ground floor. There were children's toys, Angela noticed, in the entrance hall, and she understood that the top of the house was let out to two young families. It was a soothing, a relaxing house, tempting her to curl up like a kitten in the long pale shag of the rug and purr through the cider. But that wore off. She hugged her knees and rocked gently back and forth, almost at home, at ease, once the probing had stopped and the boundaries had been understood. She saw warning and cut off if the topic turned to the Dawsons, saw it in a glance when the pale eyes turned cold. Strangely, the woman had stopped being old or severe, just Clara, with whom she could talk easily outside the limits of what she had to protect, and she was overjoyed to be returning on Friday, a reprieve from a kept-warm meal. Then she could count the days to the end, and make an effort to heal the atmosphere and make the last days of her visit pleasant for the grandparents.

But it was hard to rebuild ease, any sort of communion, between herself and her grandmother, whose tones were now habitually whines and whose glances all seemed loaded with suspicion.

"You're wasting away to nothing and I'm sure it's not my fault," she nagged on Friday morning as Angela picked at her dry breakfast toast, looking past the milk bottle and the greasy butter dish, past her grandmother to the sparrow on the window ledge, trying to be diverted from the reprimand in the air. "It's a good job you have to wear them smocks to work in so the customers don't know they're being served by a skeleton."

Grandfather came in behind her, up unusually early for him. "Ah, lay off the girl, Doris. You nagging won't help put any flesh on her. Anyhow, old lady," he wheedled her fondly, "girls aren't so plump like they used to be, ain't nothing much to love up to any more. Come on, me duck, pour us a cup o' tea."

Angela smiled for him, glad he was there as a buffer.

"Grandmother," she said quietly, hoping to have caught a good moment while she stirred the old man's tea, "don't keep dinner for me today. Mrs. Jonason, down the road, asked me down for dinner with her."

She had said the wrong thing. She knew by the way Grandmother cracked the spoon down on the oilcloth and slopped the tea in the saucer as she pushed it crossly across to Grandpa. She heard the long suck-in of air before the explosion. "She's no Missis, let me tell you. Whatever she might have told you. I have thanked my God every night that that woman was not around to lay her hands on you. Missis! Indeed! Some Missis. Her!

"She didn't tell me," Angela tried to defend.

"Now I suppose she's getting her hands on you, is she? She was always trying to get our Dinah down there. How dare she!

And her a woman like that. She never was any good. Missis, indeed. That's a good one. Her a Missis. She brought that poor little boy of hers into the world—an illegitimate. Poor little bastard."

Grandfather broke in in his quiet, reasonable, smiling way lighting a cigarette up and puffing between phrases. "It is true, what your grandmother says, Angela me duck. She never did have a husband and she was brazen about it. Some foreigner was the father of her boy. No, she isn't a good woman, Angela me duck." Grandfather shook his head and smiled at her sadly.

She looked from one to the other of the old people and didn't know what to say, so she looked down at the crumbs on the green oilcloth and pushed them together with one finger.

Grandmother was off again. "But I suppose you'll go down there whatever we say. It was the same with your mother, we couldn't keep her away from that woman. Better things down there than we've got up here, no doubt. But there is one thing I am sure of; we could have had the same things if I'd had a fancy man to provide for me. Believe me she had got herself a fancy man with money, trust her. He never wanted for anything, didn't that Jeffrey — except for a respectable father, the poor little bastard."

Would it never stop! Angela stood up and brushed herself down, picked up her shoulder bag, managing not to say anything, managing to keep her expression empty, withdrawn. "I have to be going," she smiled and backed towards the door try to leave peacefully. But it was no good. Grandmother started with renewed hysteria. "That woman. I wouldn't be surprised if that wasn't where your mother got her ideas from. A woman like that! She certainly didn't get her dirty ideas in this house. I could never have been that sort of woman. Somebody gave our Dinah the idea of going away and finding herself a man old enough to be her father. Dirty. Dirty old man! I suppose she thought she was on a good thing getting somebody old enough to have money."

Please God. Don't let me shout. Please God. She tried to control her voice. It came out full of breath, hissing, "You can't keep on about my father like that." Her own words sounded impotent to herself. Grandpa was looking at her sadly through his cigarette smoke and nodding his head from side to side. "My father," she kept saying like an idiot. "You never think a good thought about anyone." Oh why don't you keep quiet, Angela. "My mother! No wonder she never came back. You drove her away!"

Grandmother screamed and, before she slammed the door, Angela saw Grandpa reach over to hold her. Then she ran down the yard and wrenched her bike out of the back gate and pedalled furiously up the hill to work, couldn't at first go into the bakery because she couldn't stop crying, rode round the block until she thought she had regained her composure and the traces of tears had dried away. But Mike Tupp never missed a thing.

"Well, wotcher Angel Face. Been crying, eh?" he greeted her at the bakehouse door all one with the welcome warm of newly baked bread and yeast. He opened his arms, "Come on, you come and tell Uncle Mike all your troubles," he said so kindly and held her so protectively against his laundry-fresh overall that she pressed her face into his shoulder and shook while he stroked her hair. "You're just making me cry," she sobbed and tried to laugh at herself, eventually pushing herself away from him and sniffing. He came out with a big white handkerchief. "Come on, my love, blow hard for Uncle Mike and you'll feel better. I bet I know what's eating you. It's that old lady Dawson, isn't it? I've heard people say no wonder your mother never came back."

She wiped her face on his handkerchief and handed it back.

"Make the girl a cup of tea," Steve called across from the ovens. "And don't you feel bad, girl. Everybody needs a good cry sometime."

"I'm getting proper soppy, aren't I?" she said with her English accent and made herself laugh. "I'm no good at coping with poor old Grandma's nagging. You're right." She fished down in her peacock bag for make-up to disguise the traces of tears, then leaned over the sink to look in the little mirror while she made up her eyes dramatically. Mike stood watching her, waiting for the kettle to boil.

"You don't have to go back to Dawsons' if it's getting that bad," he said. "Come home with me tonight. My Mum would give you a bed. Heart of gold, my Mum. She'd give anything to have a girl around—especially a looker, like you."

"Especially one with tear-rimmed eyes and blotchy cheeks," she sniffed and raised her eyes tragically to the ceiling like a Christian martyr. "Don't be so nice, Mike. You'll make me cry again. But you know I couldn't do that. It would kill the grandparents, really hurt their feelings. I shouldn't let myself get mad at them. I'm mad at myself for getting mad, if you see what I mean."

"Don't let it worry you, girl." Steve came over to the table. "Pour a cup for me, eh Mike? My Beaty tells me your mother had some rough times and nobody was surprised when she never came back from Canada—except for the Jonason boy. People reckoned she'd a married him."

"When's Beaty arriving?" she asked to get herself out of the focus of the two men's contemplations.

"The Saturday after this one coming. She might just get to see you before you go."

Oh no, seared through Angela's mind and she pushed her hands in on her waist, tight in its girdle. Oh no, she'd see a difference after being away for two months, see changes. She would know.

"You just wait," Mike was going on and laughing, "I bet we'll hear nothing but Shirl and the baby for the first week. Can't imagine Shirl with a baby, can you, Steve?"

"Imagine her? Can't imagine me, if you ask me, with a bleedin' cobber for a grandson. Imagine the lip we'll get when he's old enough to come to visit. Worse with their tongues than us. Proper buggers them Aussies. Beaty says she's bringing back a bit of christening cake for all of us. I ask you, bringing christening cake half way round the world to a baker's!"

"Poor Rita doing all the work while we loll in here," Angela sighed and got up to go into the shop. "Do I look all right now?" she asked them.

"Better than ever, Snowbird," Mike patted her behind as she moved away.

"Don't let it worry you, girl," Steve smiled across at her as she pushed through the door into the bright shop, into bright talk, into another day with the girdle biting, another day to count against the days to the end of the two months, the time to escape.

Counting the days, sucking in and holding her breath inside the girdle whenever anyone seemed to be looking; hardly eating, hardly drinking, to stay as thin as a girl; talking blithely back to the jabber of the customers, and counting the days. Wishing the evening with Clara Jonason could last for ever— but counting the days and easing the girdle round her thighs. A last Sunday outing with Mike, tea with his nice mother and father in a prim, properly polished suburban house with heart-of-gold kindness and an artificial fireplace glowing in the hearth for the cheerful look of the thing. Listening, contemplating, when she was tired, wavering, while Mike argued, protested, pleaded that she could marry him. Kind, generous Mike! "Come on Angie. I'm twenty-five and know what I want. Old enough for both of us. I make good money."

Counting the days while Grandma could behave as though there had been no tension, no hard words, talking about the next visit and the things to be sure to tell our Dinah.

Counting the days, and going up to bed early to get out of the misery of the girdle, sit propped up by the apple-box bookshelves with the dragon shawl wrapped all around her, filling the third exercise book, the pages of the journal of this special summer, while the old men coughed and hacked and toilets flushed and gurgled noisily. Old Madeleine has been taken to hospital. I was glad. Am glad. Pray she won't be back till I am gone. How about that for iniquity, Mr. Olson?

Mr. Olson, it is almost quiet in my mind now I can count the days to when I can be a traveller in free orbit again. Except there is a screech on track eight. Track eight is binding on the spools, fit to break. Mike Tupp is on track eight now because I haven't used him right. He has been so good to me—and I am counting the days to get away. My grandfather has been so kind—and I am counting the days. My grandmother—my father—worse than counting the days—I have despised them. Track eight screeches so I have to stop my ears and look away.

Then there are the sparrows. Who will feed the sparrows when I am gone? Birds at the window, and I shall not be there. Why is it a sad thought?

My flight bag is packed and the case my mother first travelled with nineteen summers ago. In that brown case, between two sheets of firm cardboard, I have packed some of my mother's work from her art folder; a beautiful pencil drawing of a man's back at the bottom of which the teacher had written "Excellent", and the painting of Clara Jonason's face that is really my face. Wherever I go I am taking them with me.

What did Damion mean it is too bad about you, Mr. Olson. I wonder.

I am counting the days.

"Leap to Death", "Tragedy on the Tracks", "Young Woman Leaps to Death from Fast Train", were the front-page headlines on the newspapers Grandmother and Grandfather insisted on buying at the station kiosk for her to take on her journey. "You'll need something to read, all that way," they said.

"And we all know what sort of a woman she would be, don't we," Grandmother sniffed, reading the headlines. "Not like our Angela. She's never do a thing like that, would you, me duck?"

"Not this morning," Angela laughed and shook out her hair, already excited by the station bustle. They stood on the platform watching for the train to come out of the grey rain of the morning. Grandmother was watery-eyed. "We are going to miss you. We've got used to having you. Don't know what we shall do without you," she kept saying and squeezing Angela's arm, while Grandfather dragged through his cigarette, lit up another, alternately watched down the track then turned to smile at his granddaughter shyly through his smokescreen. "You see and come again, me duck. I'll be keeping the bike oiled and polished for you."

At the last minute Mike came into the station and brought her a box of chocolates, big and expensive. "Remember I'm here if you need me," he said as he hefted her baggage onto the rack.

Then she was waving to them as the train pulled away. Then they were small puppets. Then they were gone. The two months had ended. Finished.

She had the railway carriage to herself and the wet towers of the city were rattling past the window, street on street, grey city, but going away, retreating. She flopped back into the corner and luxuriously stretched her legs along the red seat. "Young Woman Leaps to Death from Fast Train", she read, and turned to look at the tracks flashing by, shining, gleaming silver in the rain, grass struggling by the tracks, city grass struggling, clackety-clack, merrily measuring the miles.

If I jumped . . .

Poor Grandma would know then. That sort of woman!

Would my mother cry?

But it isn't grey out there in the slow fall of the rain. It is silver. Silver England. And there's a little boy making waves in a long puddle, waves spreading outward as the train leaves him behind. No, she doesn't feel like jumping from the train.

Like Grandmother says, "She'd never do a thing like that."

Instead she undid the waist of her pants, let the zipper down and lay back with her hands cupping the small bulge of her belly pressed under the harsh elastic grip of the girdle. She put her cheek against the plush of the carriage seat, curled her knees up to her and let herself rock to the motion of the train, in the luxury of being safely carried in the impersonal private cosiness of the carriage.

Up on the rack there, there was more than half of a boat label left on the old brown suitcase, left from its very first journey nineteen years and one month ago. Her mother must have sat on a train to Liverpool, rocking, rocking, watching the case on the rack above.

The city had given way to silver-lawned suburbs and doll-houses with mirror-wet roofs and mirror-wet streets. Somebody running with a red umbrella.

In the red flight bag, under the shoes, zippered down in a flowered plastic toilet bag, eight weeks' wages are stashed away.

And she still has the travellers' cheques in the little book from the little bank in the little town, intact except for the one she cashed at the airport that very first day. A hundred and fifty dollars untouched—saved from another lifetime ago. How many lifetimes ago?

From the insides of the peacock bag she fished up a battered red plastic-covered address book, a Christmas present from a girl when she was in grade six. From between its pages she took the folded sheet of green notepaper, a smooth printed card and the small side of a confectioner's box, spreading the three on the seat. Sam the American's sharp tilted pencil-written address to his smidgin of a basement flat. "Jeffrey Jonason" printed in quality printing and a reminder underneath his address, in Clara's plain hand, "September 6th at 7 p.m."

Two children walked down the corridor and looked in her compartment. She pulled her blouse down quickly to cover the gap in her pants' opening and got up to slide the door along. Closed.

The train was skittering now fast across the rain-drenched countryside.

Funny, she could only think of Jeffrey Jonason as the white-haired boy in her grandmother's snapshots, as the high-school boy holding her mother's bike. Funny, addresses of two violinists. Funny.

Mike had printed his address and a phone number and underneath written, "anytime, day or night".

She folded them together carefully and put them back in the childish address book, next to the cover where her own childish handwriting said "If this book should ever roam, smack its bum and send it home to Angela Moynahan, Gladden, Alberta, Canada, North America, Western Hemisphere, The World, The Universe." Home.

She put the address book back in her bag, then took it out again. She took the folded addresses, let the train window down, leaned out into the rain and tore them into broken pieces, letting them scatter slowly, bit by bit, into the whip of the wind, the remains of other lives. She let the wind take her hair and buffet her face, held out her hands and her arms into the wet of the fall of the rain. It felt good.

Then she lurched and laughed with the sway of the train to the cramped rocking lavatory where she took off the girdle. Breathed freely. Pulled her blouse well down over the bulge and the pull round her pants.

Back in her compartment, behind the closed door, she opened the window again, flung the undergarment into the wind, never saw it land.

She might as well eat the chocolates.

Now she was on her own. She could cope.

She was certain she could get lost somewhere in the vast spread of London. It was exciting to be back.

On arrival she checked her luggage in at the station and jaunted freely around the streets until she found a bed-and-breakfast place that looked dingy enough to be cheap. When she pulled the yellow net curtains apart she looked across dreary stacks of unpainted thin old houses to the white clock-face of a spiring church; diadem rising from city fungus, she thought, and laughed. It was good to be free.

All night the clock chimed on the hour and she counted the chimes, sometimes turned to smile and look across the calm darkness of its steady face. Serene sentinel.

The morning smell of bacon was for her, a sure signal to get up and choose coffee at a nice enough table, and only have to say a polite "Good morning" to the shabby men who breakfasted silently behind their newspapers. A table of private worlds, each intact in this oasis. A sanctuary of non-interference. Then she could pay the bill and leave again. Free.

Sun again, into a London morning, shafting gold and tossing sunbeams like bubbles on blackened brick walls, so she swung her peacock bag and ran across the shadows to make the most of the streaks of morning warm.

When she came to a bus station she took a bus that was filling up rapidly, took a chance that it was going to the sort of place she wanted, and when the woman on the seat in front asked for a four-and-sixpenny ticket, she asked for the same, not knowing really where she was going till she got there. A teeming place, that's what she wanted, but away from the centre, a place to find a cheap place to live, work, a place that looked to have enough of its own troubles without involving itself in hers. She watched out of the bus window, marvelling at the town on town on town that she thought of as London. She got off in what seemed to be the main street of what looked like the

128

busiest and shabbiest of the places the bus had gone through.

Towards the end of the day she found a flat in a reasonably respectable narrow street with tall houses. It was a small room, the only one in use in the attic of the old Georgian house that was now owned by a faded old Italian gentleman, who explained to her that the other rooms up there needed so much doing to them that it wasn't worth his while to rent them out. There were two other rooms. They weren't locked. He said if anything in them was any use to her she could help herself, then he went slowly backwards down the winding narrow attic staircase, leaving her to make herself at home.

A smidgin of a flat in a back-street United Nations! She danced around on the blue linoleum, then looked up at the small high window, too grimed to let in even the sky. She pushed the old brass-bedsteaded bed heavily over to the window and climbed up to look out, rubbed a hole through the inside dirt to let in through the grimed rain-runs of the other side a vista of roofs and chimneys with the long shadows of the late sun. The window wouldn't open so she went into one of the other rooms where junk had collected under a fallen ceiling, and found a heavy chair leg. With it she rammed and levered the little window open, and leaned out to look down past the roofs to the backyards and streets in the well of life at the bottom. Never a tree, no grass. But the sunshine making long shadows.

In the little dark kitchen that was hers she found a rag to clean off the window. Then the sunlight broke across her yellow ceiling. It was not so bad. If she polished the brass on the bed. Her peacock bag where she had flung it on the seat of the stuffed brown chair was a bright patch. The blue linoleum was comparatively new. A gas fire with a meter for shillings and an old brown standard lamp by the old brown chair. She switched the lamp on. It worked, gave a brown glow. That was nice. A cream-painted wooden table and kitchen chair looked hospital-like. She left the lamp on for when she got back because it would be dark, and she searched and inquired and waited for a bus to take her back to the station to get her luggage and bring it home.

It wasn't bad, at all.

She spread her dragon shawl across the bed, and with the brass nobbles shining—there was something to look at, especially when a streak of sun fell in. And by some miracle, there was a library, a massive old library just a short walk away. The Italian landlord signed the form so she could join. Three books at a time meant that she could borrow two with bright covers, the biggest and brightest, and use them to make gay on the table, on the arm of the chair, on the blue linoleum down by the fire. It was cosy at night with the fire bubbling and smelly warm, and the brown lamp making a pool of glow. She pinned her mother's sketches on the wall, moved them from place to place, trying to find the best place for them to be positive on so much dingy bare wall. She settled for putting them low, by the side of the fireplace, the face with her eyes above the drawing marked "Excellent".

It wasn't bad at all. In fact it was very peaceful. She enjoyed pottering in the windowless cubbyhole of a kitchen with its deep brown cupboard and a gas stove blackened by a thousand years of meals, it seemed. She closed the doors on the other two rooms because it was creepy at night when the house creaked and stretched through the silence. Sometimes she met other people on the stairs, people who just nodded and went on their own way. Working people she thought. Not old. The landlord, Mr. Isseppi, sometimes met her at the door to ask, "Is everything all right?" He never bothered her. She became part of the place, inhabiting it quietly, coming and going with her own key to the door; the fair one in the attic.

She wrote a note to Clara Jonason saying she wouldn't be there for dinner, addressed it to Clara's own home, down the alley from her grandmother.

She arranged for a florist to deliver a dozen red roses for her grandparents and wrote a note saying she was going to be travelling. She imagined the roses next to the milk bottle, the bread, and the butter dish, singing out their perfume.

Twenty minutes' walk away there was a post office in the next postal district to the one she was living in, and it was to this one she asked her mother to send her mail, poste restante. I shall be youth-hostelling around she wrote, then tore that letter up and wrote another that simply said travelling. Her father would be humiliated to think of her hostelling—because he had never done it to know what it was.

She felt she was making herself safe from discovery. Even in the bathtub, two floors down, in the gurgle and steam of the fierce geyser that flung out boiling water dangerously into the middle of the tub so she crouched at the end for safety, even soaking in the tub, in the luxury of the endless hot water (endless because she put her own coins in the meter to the geyser), she felt safe. A part of the romance of the city. It was very peaceful.

She started her new job the beginning of the next week, at the large dry-cleaners a ten-minute walk away from home. She was a presser, working away from the public, needing only to talk to her immediate boss, Silvia, a mature West Indian woman. The two of them had the work area, the steam, the pressing job to themselves. "Don't you worry about a thing. I'll teach you everything there is to know," Silvia promised the day Angela asked for the job, and was as good as her word. In no time at all Angela was whipping shirts on and off the shirt press, expertly pulling and turning garments in between the massive industrial steam pads, soon expert enough to watch the back-street activities going on and passing by the large store-type window in which they worked. Sometimes children stood at the window watching them work. Silvia laughed. "Must be something for them to watch. Me so black and you so white. The witch and the fairy—eh?" And she laughed big in her generous chest.

Not that Silvia talked much. The garments hissed and Silvia hummed deep and far away, working peacefully, rhythmically, in the tropics of the steam room, and warm September slipped into cooler October, peacefully.

"You need to rest your legs, honey," Silvia insisted quietly and brought in an extra chair for her to put her feet up when they took their breaks. "Now look here, I can make the tea. I can run around the corner and get the chips. You rest up, honey, when you get the chance." No questions. No advice beyond that.

At the end of September Angela used two weeks' wages to buy a cape she saw on sale in a good store, a beautiful woollen thing, brown and gold plaid with a gold lining. It was more practical than a maternity coat, she thought, and she felt stylish in it rather than pregnant. As soon as she had it she went to Canada House to collect the mail that would have been sent there before she gave her mother the poste restante address. She had waited till she had the cape as her disguise. She might have met someone from home.

The same neatly written news from home, almost the same every time. The constant of home. Harvest was in except for the oats. Gordon had done most of the work this year because her father didn't seem at all well, very tired. Dinah was having an exhibition in Edmonton, but the house seemed bare with all the wall hangings down. She had been asked to show her work in Winnipeg. It was so exciting. Her father wrote at the bottom, "What do you think of your mother getting famous? Be a good girl". And he scrawled four untidy kisses. Gordon always sent his love. One sentence at the end of a letter said that Mr. Olson wasn't coming back to the school.

Then there was the parcel from Mr. Olson, so long on its way. She smiled tiredly as she opened it under the light of the high window of her attic; a book, *Women Poets of Canada*. How like him to have written inside just under the title, "for more than one springtime", taking her starkly back to the classroom with snow at the window flying and a bird crashing —when her belly was flat. There were no birds at the attic window. There was no ledge. She had never put out any bread. But tomorrow she would.

A short note from Mr. Olson, with no address, said that she was one of his last students. He was finished with teaching. "Enough is enough in this one little life", he had written, knowing she would remember phrases from before. "My wife and I have decided to spend a year bumming round Europe remembering our springtime, when we did it once before."

In the old brown chair in the lamp's brown glow, with the gas fire her own cosiness, she read back into the ragged snow through the poets in the book, her women, barbed, not smoothed, into loveliness. Mr. Olson, thank you.

She unearthed exercise book four from the bottom of her flight bag, made a bun necklace to hang outside the window, hung it on a nail rammed in with the chair leg. But no birds came.

There are no birds at this window. I have not written since I came here because I am a vegetable and it is very peaceful. You were right about the big belly; it would not be elegant to travel with. It moves under my hands but I keep it out of my head, so, you see, I don't know what I intend to do with it. A lot of things don't happen to me any more. I see them and know they are there, but they don't happen to me. I found a park a long walk away, a rough park left with last year's leaves. They blow and I watch them. They blow across the tramped-out place in the grass by the children's swings—but not in me. I only watch, as I watch the steam and the whites of Silvia's eyes and the thin legs of poor city children outside the window. I think I know how it was that my mother never cried. I don't think I shall ever know how to cry again. But it is very peaceful. I sleep a lot and will not dream.

Blowing in the wind, tapping at the window, the necklace of buns gathered soot, got wet, then dried out again. It was a slummy thing but she didn't take it down, she just came and went, the fair one in the attic, leaning backwards under the autumn cape, drifting like steam carrying the faint chemical scent of the dry-cleaners.

The first Sunday in November she was up early to get the bathroom to soak away the weariness and chemicals of the week and was lying in the weekend luxury of bubble bath, watching the steam turn to drops and run ribbons down the tall window, two storeys below her own, when she heard the gulls. There was no mistaking the cries. The same cries behind a tractor at home, circling for worms. Gulls' cries. What did they do to her? Crying through her? She left the water to run away and with her towels bundled she raced up to her room to stand on the bed and look out of the window. Two gulls, wheeling and shrieking. Swooping down to take cruel lunges at the old necklace, stabbing it, breaking it, filling the window with their wings. Visitors, like gods. Then one grabbed too savagely and the whole thing, buns, string and nail, pulled away, and the gull soared with the necklace hanging from its beak. Angela laughed out loud and opened the window to lean

133

out and watch the birds go, the one behind swooping and screaming. The gulls came up from the river and found my window. Now they will come every morning and I shall feel like somebody special. Such life at the window!

In the second week of November there were blue circles under her eyes and Silvia watched her as she raised and lowered the great pressing-pad. A blue vein was showing behind the knee in one long leg and tracing a line down her calf.

"When's your baby due, honey?"

"January," she sighed. "It takes such a long time."

"You should quit work while you're still winning, honey. You're getting tired."

Angela paused in her pressing, smoothed a wrinkle from the bright orange of the cloth, looked vaguely out of the window into the twilight under the street lights. "Such a long time left to sit around yet—and—" she moved quickly, brought the top of the presser down, and bent herself behind the equipment.

"What did you see? Are you all right?" Silvia looked out at the people looking in, then back at Angela. "You know them, that old couple? Honey, are you all right?"

"Were they looking?"

"Sure they were looking. Hey, honey, sit down, you've gone as white as your hair."

The girl at the front desk yelled back loudly, "Hey, Silvia. Do we have an Angela back there?"

"No sir," Silvia answered in the deep voice and accents of a big black momma. "No sir. We done only got a Georgina and a Silvie. No Angela ever been back here. No sir." She put her good wide self between Angela and the window, held up a big curtain to fold it.

"They are from my home," Angela whispered, remembering that Mary Ellis had gone to Canada as a war bride. "Dear God, they must have relatives here."

"Why don't you slip out the back way, honey, in case they look in again. It's nearly time." Silvia was conspiratorial, understanding everything.

Behind the rack of clothes Angela pulled her cape around her, buttoning her hair, her tell-tale hair, down inside. And her fingers were shaking. Silvia was humming loudly. Her knitted red hat was on a chair. Angela grabbed the hat and pulled it down over her head. Down almost covering her eyes and she ran out by the back door, past the garbage cans, down the back alley, running, running, pulling the hat down, holding it, pulling it as she ran, her arms bare white reaching up out of the slits of the cape. She ran and ran, taking the back alleys, away from her own street, ran in the shadows, avoiding the pools of yellow under the street lamps. She dodged into dark doorways seeing in every approaching face an Ellis, a neighbour from home.

She dodged and hid again, ran and hid again, bending in doorways, ran again under the red knitted hat until it was night and properly dark. Then she dodged from shadow to shadow till she saw the library, her library. The Ellises would never be in a library. Sanctuary. She fled into the reading room among the old men hidden behind newspapers, picked up a paper and held it close to her face and lay back gasping in a leather chair. The paper would not keep still. It shook.

"Is he after you, miss?" A yellow hand plucked at the top of the paper, cataracted old man's eyes loomed over the rim at her, a tobacco-wet old mouth laughed, "Is he after you? Eh—eh—eh?"

She held her breath and stared vacant-eyed at the tears running over the red rims of the ancient eyes.

"You're reading it upside down," the head nodded and cackled, and cackled—

She ran again. Pulled the hat right down. Looked for the lights through the knitting. Crept round the streets inside under the hat until she saw her house through the knitting. Then she ran for the door and hammered with both her fists.

"Missy. Missy." The old Italian landlord took her hat off gently, unbuttoned her cape and led her into his warm kitchen, sat her by his fire, stood over her while she drank down a long shot of brandy, stroked her hair murmuring, "Missy. Missy."

"You get into bed, missy. I'll be up and bring you a good drink, something to make you sleep—good."

He laboured up the last stairs with a hot-water bottle as well as a mug of hot milk laced with rum and sugar.

"Drink it all up, missy," he urged her, and kept one hand under the mug to still its shaking between her fingers, so suddenly frail and pale. "Then you just lie down, go to sleep, missy. Not to worry about a thing. I'll look in, keep an eye on you." He tucked the blankets up round her shoulders and smoothed the dragon shawl. Then she was asleep in the deep warm with the hot-water bottle held against her red nightie.

The water bottle had chilled off when the pain came but she still clutched it as she moved to ease herself into another position. It had gone, the pain. She turned over into the moonlight slitting in through the high window. Moon shadow on her ceiling, window bars and a length of string blowing, laid bare of its bread by the seagulls. The pain again, aching, growing, tearing down her back, and the thing inside beating against her hands, and the pain dying into an ache, and her hands gone cold, clutching the tepid water bottle to the aching base at the root of her belly. The pain again, coming, gathering, then subsiding. She groaned with the wave of the pain, because she was alone, herself talking to herself. "What shall I do?" she moaned and watched the string shadow swinging across the moonlight on the wall. These are the pains. It is happening.

She got up and lit the gas fire, sat crouching over its orange, blue-edged glow in the moon-shafted dark waiting for the pains. Perhaps they would go away. Perhaps she was mistaken. What now? She hadn't made a place in her mind yet for this. No, the pains were not going to go away. They were coming with harsher groaning force. She must get dressed.

She folded her night things, pushed them down into her

peacock bag with *Women Poets of Canada*, she put her toothbrush in—then that was that.

She made her bed straight, put out the light again, and sat on the linoleum floor by the fire leaning against the old armchair with her cape on, ready to go. She put her face into the worn plush of the chair-seat and gasped as the pains came and took her. But where was she to go? She hadn't made a place in her mind for this yet. She hadn't thought where to go. She bit into the old plush of the brown chair and moaned.

"Missy. Missy," he whispered and opened the door letting in a corridor of light from the stairway. "Oh missy. You bad? You were sound asleep last time I looked." He stood in the strip of light from the stairway, not seeming like her landlord, him so little with thin ankles bare above sloppy slippers, pyjamas ghost-striped in the stripe of light, his dressing-gown hanging.

"Missy," he said, going over to her and bending. She stood up, taller than him, a mountain in the cape. He didn't seem like her landlord, this man with rumpled night hair, a grey fringe of rumpled curls, and his hands very long out of the sleeves of his dressing-gown.

She clutched the back of the chair and bit her lip, doubled over into the pain. He bent down too and looked up into her face. "You need to go to hospital, missy?" His glasses were blind discs. She breathed hard, unevenly.

"I go phone for the ambulance, okay?" he asked gently with a hand on hers on the back of the chair. So it was easy. Go phone for an ambulance.

"A few minutes, missy, and it'll be here, the ambulance. Come on down. Okay. Okay. I'll lock your door. Don't worry about nothing. I give you a drink while you wait."

Again he put hot rum in a tall mug and steadied it between her cold hands while she sipped it down into the vacant abyss where the pains gathered like storms and shrieked through the gully of her back. Warm rum. Sweet in the mouth that is divorced from the pain, cloudy in the head that listens to the pain roaring and sways as it follows the path of the fury.

Hands took her arms and voices soothed her into the ambulance and the city lights flashed and flickered and played patterns into her eyes. Patterns nothing to do with the pain that was happening somewhere else down under a blanket, while the lights sped through the city.

She closed her eyes against the questions that faces asked with typewriters against their fingers. She closed her eyes and swayed her head from side to side. No doctor. No next of kin. No religion. No husband. No. No. No. . . . They took her clothes off and bathed her in tepid water and tied her in a white gown and shaved off her pubic hair and the summer-gold hair from her thighs. She closed her eyes, against the hands that pushed and pressed and felt, and against the voices that questioned, then talked across her, across the heels walking, hurrying down long corridors, pushing her and the pain on wheels down long corridors with women crying out down the sides.

"Mrs. Moynahan, Mrs. Moynahan," the voices kept saying, shouting through her closed eyes. "Call if you need anything. There's a microphone by your bed. A little shot to ease the pain. A little sleep, Mrs. Moynahan." Round the edges of the sleep, women crying desolate cries through her sleep like coyotes wailing on the edges of her prairie. Then women cursing and grunting like sows in the pig barn. Women crying out to God, crying for their mothers, cursing their husbands.

So this is pain. A flame lashing out and pulling the brain down into the hiss of the fire, hiss and scream, fall into the furnace exploding behind the eyes. Close the eyes. There is no one to call out to. Behind the eyes, alone with the sear of the firework that is my body consuming my brain. Explode like a firework, red and blue and white shafts breaking through the back of closed eyes. Fall into the firework. Explode inwards. Make not a sound. There is no one. This is the moment of being. The brain is in the pain. The belly explodes through the eyes and is sucked in again by the tongue of the flame that is pulling me into the white heat of the splitting firework.

Close the eyes, the voices are prodding and hand are pressing and pushing and diving between her legs and up into the pain. And the heels are running along the hard corridor pushing the pain on wheels and hands are pushing and rolling and lifting and the light is a pain through the eyelids making her turn her head to the side.

138

"Mrs. Moynahan. Mrs. Moynahan," the voices are shouting through the pain. "With the next pain, bear down, mother." Someone is holding her hand and she holds it desperately, afraid she'll hurt it when the pain grabs and the voices insist, "Bear down, mother. Bear down." Mother. Mother. Mother. Close her eyes against the words.

She pulled the hand to her cheek. Then the pain again. But a battle. Push against the pain. Drive it down. Drive it out. Close her eyes against the voices, talking her down from the pain. It's broken, the pain. "Pant, mother, pant." It's gone. The pain. And the thing, a warm banana skin against her thighs. Warm and wet, lying on her thighs. The hand takes itself out of her hand. The voices have stopped and the lights are humming. A man is breathing hard. She puts her arm across her eyes to shade them from the humming lights, fierce lights.

To breathe without pain.

A cool hand pressed again on her stomach. A hand held her hand again and a voice coming out of the lights was gentle. "It's all over. All over, Mrs. Moynahan. Open your eyes Mrs. Moynahan. It's all over."

But she kept her eyes closed and tossed her head to the other side away from the hand that held her hand. For a moment she looked under her lashes across the white light to the white uniforms. Three uniforms. One is holding the baby up by the heels, pale waxen thing with black hair. A hand smacks its little wax bottom. Three bent faces whispered gravely. She closed her eyes again, turned her head back to the hand holding her hand.

Close out the waxen baby. With black hair.

"I'm afraid your baby is very sick," the voice above the hand said. Said it so carefully. Careful to be careful.

"Dead?" Angela opened her eyes briefly to look up into the neat cool face of the nurse with the hand holding on to her hand and the face, very neat, looking out of dark eyes with careful compassion, nodding sadness.

Close out the waxen baby. Long hair black on its neck. Close out the sadness in the careful eyes. Fall back into the empty furnace where the fireworks were. Fall. Fall into warm and wheels and heels down long corridors. Fall.

139

"Damn you. Will you open your eyes?" Someone is pulling her up by the shoulders, shaking her. Somebody isn't gentle.

She opened her eyes. No harder than opening them under water. Just open them. There were blue eyes, dark, glowering back out of a young man's face with its straight brown hair rumpled, sticking up. She saw past the young man to the nurses at the bottom of the bed and her feet down there, bare, thin. Blood on her feet. She closed her eyes again. Blood on feet. A waxen baby with a clenched fist. With black hair, held by the ankles. Fall back into the fireworks. Fall into the warm.

"Damn you, woman. Open your eyes." She was warm in the blankets. He shook her up by the shoulders.

"Stop it," she said and looked back into his troubled eyes. Blue. Dark. His white coat was open and he was sitting on her bed.

"Will you make an effort, woman?" he said. "Look at me." He shook her again. "Make an effort. It's bad enough to lose a baby. Come on, get with it. I can't afford to lose a mother."

"Does it matter?" she asked watching the lines round his mouth.

"It matters to me," he said.

"It's a nice colour," she said and traced her finger across the cables in the knit of his sweater. "Like a wheat field at harvest," she said.

"My mother knit it. I'm sorry about the baby."

I would like to meet a man like you, her mind thought shockingly, you make me feel safe. The mind won't stay on grief. Your hair sticks up like a little boy's and your eyes are clever, not pretending.

"I'm sorry about the baby. Why don't you cry?"

"It's a very nice colour," she said back in the twist of the knitting. "You must have a very nice mother."

"I have. Why won't you cry? Cry, woman."

Why would he want her to cry? He has very clever eyes. Can't he tell she doesn't want to cry?

"Woman, pull yourself together. Snap out of it. Don't go away," he said and shook her again. She smiled at the line of his tense jaw and at the trouble in his eyes. Clever eyes. "I got a scholarship," she said, trying to reach him where the eyes were clever.

"I'm sorry about the baby," he said again.

"Don't be."

"Hell, it is my job."

"I won't die," she said and smiled. "At least I'm flat." She spread her hands on the bedcover where her bulge had been. "Honest I won't die."

"You're sure about that, eh?"

"I just want to sleep."

"Don't you want to cry?"

"No."

He stood up by the bed and looked puzzled. She leaned back on the pillows and met his gaze seriously, tried to explain. "I haven't worked out what to cry for yet. Who would you cry for?"

"I'll send you to sleep," he said.

It was nearly the end of November when they let her out of hospital, back to her room where Silvia's red knitted hat was still on the tired brown chair where she'd left it, violent. She was all right now, free, and with enough money. In hospital they had put her in a room away from the cries of the babies, so she'd get over the experience, and the nurses who took her pulse had made talk telling her she could have lots more babies. Except one nurse, the one who had rammed the painful injection into her bottom to take away the milk. That one had slapped her on the bruise where she'd rammed in the needle. "Nothing's wasted," she had said. "You'll make something of the experience. What are you reading?"

On the first afternoon she went out, hugging her cape into the thin unfamiliarity of her body, a thin mist silvered the streets and feathered the unreality of her weakness. She bought a long-stemmed yellow rose at the florist's for Mr. Isseppi, the landlord, and held it across her arm in its sheath of white wrapping. As in a dream she sat in a café, sat in the window at a white-clothed table pulling her stomach in and trying to pull the drifting world outside the window back sharp into focus into her head. People edged with mist, vaguely passing. Enough money at the bottom of her bag, but you can't sit forever at a café table sniffing the three red carnations with their wisp of fern. People outside in the mist, like a painting, unreal. Unreal to be free. Unreal. But push the slender vase with the red carnations back to the centre of the white cloth where they all belong, and walk out light into the mist, a yellow rose cradled in white wrapping softly, softly on her arm. She stopped by a shop window to look at herself in a mirror, lifted her chin and stared haughtily into her own eyes, very big with blue rings round them, and the face severe with hollows in the cheeks. "So, you're a monster," she said to her eyes and lifted her chin harder, walked away making herself remember the flame and the pain and the furnace exploding and the waxen baby with crinkled buttocks under the handslap, and the little arm bent, with clenched fist, and black hair. They had told her it was a girl. "We blessed her and called her Angelina," the nurse who was so careful to be careful with the patient's feelings had said sadly out of her neat face, "and she was buried, a little part of another funeral in a quiet graveyard." A part of me left to be forever England. Left. Alone.

In the crinkle of the white wrapping the yellow rose was velvet and perfume escaping, and she was free, light, reborn to take off and travel to yellow sand and hot summer, somewhere, reprieved. For more than one springtime, Mr. Olson. See.

She collected her mail from the poste restante office but was afraid to open the three letters from home. People can be born, dead, and buried in less time than she had been in hospital. The Ellises could have had time to send letters, or time to have gone back and told everybody what they had seen in a back-street dry-cleaners. But now, anyhow, she could prove they were mistaken, couldn't she?

She put off opening the letters. Three airletters from her mother with the Canada Goose flying unspoiled, clean. Her mother addressed them so carefully, writing small to leave the goose flying free. Her mother. But she didn't want to open the letters.

First she gave Mr. Isseppi the rose that made tears spill on his cheeks, then she strung out bread to bring back the seagulls, made herself coffee so the attic smelled like home, lit the gas fire. Then she opened the letters, beginning with the first in order as they had been postmarked with the rubber stamp in the little post office at Gladden.

News of home continuing in pattern; such a mild November. The cattle still in the far pasture. Just as well because her father was so very tired. Damion had been in to say goodbye and said to be remembered to her. Really he had worked up quite an excitement for the North now, said he was going to see as much of it as he could while he had the chance. Gordon sent his love and her father was not at all well. Gordon sent his love and they were going to have to take her father to see a doctor.

The last letter was short. "We have had to take your father to hospital. I waited for the results of the tests before I wrote. Angela, darling, he is very sick. I don't know what to write to you. Do you want to come home? He asks every day if there is a letter from you. It is a while since we heard from you but I suppose you have been very busy doing something exciting."

Her insides caved in and she felt the blood flow again, and the gulls were already screaming at the window while she packed. Dear God, thanks for taking my belly. She could never have gone—like that. So quick, the leaving. Library books and the red hat for Mr. Isseppi to see to, and his rent paid, and his room given back empty of her visit. No, she couldn't wait. No, not phone, she had to be on her way, waiting constructively outside her own life at the airport with planes coming and going, rocking the night, spilling purposeful people into distraction all around her, she was with her hair newly washed for the last time in the geyser-gushing bathtub, hair a scented curtain where she sat on the red flight bag bent over the soreness of her insides, waiting for the plane whose time of arrival she had stated clearly in the telegram. Arriving Calgary, Wednesday afternoon, two forty-five. Span the world. Leave me behind in an attic room where the gulls come crying, in an ambulance forever crossing the night, in a hospital room, in an English graveyard where I never went to look.

Time swooned into weakness. Follow the crowd and do as the air hostess said, air hostess swaying like a nurse. Swallow the food and look at the back of the seat in front. Flames flung out of wings like fireworks sizzling, like a furnace exploding, and she bought rum, Mr. Isseppi's comfort to warm the mind, to ease it off track eight, Mr. Olson. Remember track eight, Mr. Olson, track eight binding, screeching, distorting the eyes, when I close my eyes to sleep, track eight binding, screaming through the drift of the dream that nods my head, then jerks me back to the eyes. Eyes. Eyes. My father's eyes pleading for a place, and my grandfather's loving, and my grandmother's bleeding, and Mike Tupp's trusting, and Clara's wanting me to dare—and a baby upside down in my eyes, screaming mute through a waxen skin, with crinkled heels, and you, Mr. Olson, stroking your beard and laughing, your eyes mocking. Mock

144

me. Track eight is slicing under the fingernails of my mind where my father is carrying me on his shoulders across the pasture, and Rory, his child, running ahead to tease the killdeer into crying. My father is my childhood, with gulls following the tractor, and rolling in the hayfield, and sitting up at night in the pig barn—my father is—he patted my horse and sent scrawled kisses, and all the time he knew I was running away glad to be leaving him. I was hating him.

I hated my father. Track eight binds on the truth, stretching guilt to breaking. And I am running back to my father because I hated him. That is the truth. I want to ease track eight from hurting. Unwind it. Climb out of nightmare into experience, smooth on a cosmetic face for Calgary coming up to meet the plane. She brushed her hair and shook herself to get the afternoon in focus.

In focus, in slow motion, she was down to earth. Gordon was there to meet her. Of course. Who else?

"Hi Gordon," she said and warned him off with her eyes while she held herself straight and walked towards the turntable that would rotate her luggage.

"There's a wind blowing. I had to park right at the other side of the car park," he told her and she tucked her hair inside her cape.

"How's my Dad?" she asked and kept her eyes on a piece of luggage stuck all over with bizarre labels.

"As well as can be expected." He sounded foreign and the pitch of the voice thin. "They're operating today. Dinah's up there now, at the hospital." She felt him watching her as she watched the luggage—turning—turning—

"What are they operating for?"

"Cancer, I guess. Stomach."

"Oh." She followed him and the easy small burden of her luggage out of the building, across the cutting wind between the cars, holding on to her cape, her hair whipping like string across her eyes. "Your truck's at the garage, getting fixed," he said and hefted her stuff into the back of his '59 G.M. The door on her side still had a stiff handle. He pushed his black hat back on his wind-shone forehead and lit up a cigarette while he let the engine warm up. "Don't lean on that door. It flies

145

open," he warned her and puffed out a cabful of smoke. "Well, did you have a good time?"

"Sure," she said and saw a trace of snow in the wind.

"Well," he tilted his head back and narrowed his eyes like a cowboy on television, "are you ready to settle down now?" She didn't say anything. He sounded foreign. She watched the procession of cars, lifeless, her fingers pushing the stuffing back in the broken place in the seat between them. "How's my mother?" she asked.

"Dinah's taking it pretty good. Joe'll be glad you're back. He didn't like you being over there. Ellises were over there." Her fingers pushed into the hole, into the lumpy padding; her insides caved in and she felt the blood flow again. "Oh," she said, eyes on the traffic.

"Yes, Ellises said they thought they saw you."

"Oh. I didn't see them." She sat up out of her waist, pushed her peacock bag over the hole and felt herself go goose pimply. "Cold?" He leaned over to turn the heating up. "Blowing cold. Looks like snow. Still we can't grumble. Been pretty mild. So far." He laughed between the phrases and she didn't help him make contact. She was in focus now. Flat focus. Cold.

Slow motion; he locked her luggage in the cab so no one would steal it, walked too near her with his hands in the pockets of his blue puffed parka, across the parking lot, in through the doors, warm gust out of the wind—in. She paused to smooth her hair back and there was her mother, without a coat, as though she lived in the hospital, neat and tailored-looking in a beige dress with a patterned silk scarf knotted loosely at the neck.

"Angela, darling." She had changed her perfume, very soft on her neck, very soft cheek to hold the moment steady against and avoid having to say words. Concentrate on steadying the legs gone suddenly tired. No, don't cry.

"Let's go and have a coffee first," Dinah said firmly and they walked side by side along the grey hospital corridor with the muffle of Gordon's windbreaker and loose boots behind. Angela took off her cape in the clatter of the cafeteria and smoothed her dark sweater down sleek over her slacks while Dinah was

at the counter getting the coffee and Gordon stood there waiting for his milkshake.

"Darling, people look so ghastly so soon after surgery,"
Dinah said, sitting down. "You must be tired; it could be
upsetting."

She's trying to warn me, Angela thought, and sat up
straighter, sipped the strong black Canadian coffee—home.
"Maybe you should wait till tomorrow."

"Is he all right?" she looked away from Gordon straddling
the chair next to her mother, his jacket hanging fat and open
like a burst cocoon. She held eyes with her mother across the
coffee, across the narrow white table, wondered what it meant
to those calm blue eyes, the thing that was happening to Joe
Moynahan. Was she calm behind the eyes? Her mother.

Everything slow. Slow motion. Dead focus. They leaned in
towards each other sipping black coffee. Gordon leaned back
on his chair with the metal milkshake tub between his two big
hands, sucking slowly through a fat straw.

"Is he conscious yet?"

"Yes. I sat with him while he came out of the anaesthetic.
He's resting now."

"Dinah's been here since eight this morning," Gordon paused
in his sucking.

"I'll go see him. By myself. You stay here with Mum, Gordon.
Room 709. Okay?" she pulled the rib of her sweater down
thin, down over her crotch and behind, walked out very tall,
Gordon gurgling up the last of his milkshake, eyeing her.

Outside room 709, Angela pulled her sweater down again
and sucked herself in hard. Her father was ready, watching the
door when she went in, watching from terrible eyes, poignant
and fierce in their paled weakness, so sunk under the white
crags of his rumpled eyebrows. She tried to hold her breath
steady, keep the smile just ordinary, not register the crawling
horror passing over her. How old he was, and the face so little
without its teeth, yellow, and the hand at the end of the bare
scrawny arm, yellow, frail. Yellow Madeleine . . .

"Oh Dad," she whispered and went over to the side where
the apparatus wasn't attached to him. "Oh Dad." She put her

hand over his and reached up the bed height to put her cheek against his sunken one, and kept it there in the close and personal stench of sick breath. How little he was.

A nurse came in. "Everything all right, Mr. Moynahan?" Cheerfully she bounced the words, bright pretence, scanning the tubes and dials attached to him as she talked. "You must be Angela, Mr. Moynahan's daughter? We've heard all about her, haven't we, Mr. Moynahan? So they found you. You got here. That's nice, isn't it, Mr. Moynahan? But don't stay long, Miss Moynahan. Don't tire him."

He turned his hand over under hers and gave a little pressure with his fingers. He started to speak, struggling in a hoarse whisper. "I knew you'd come." He swallowed and struggled with the jerk of the bone that was his adam's apple. "I knew it wasn't true, what the Ellis woman said." The words were so hoarse, so struggled for. "Be a good girl. Settle down now. Good girl." He held her fingers. The words so difficult.

"Sure Dad, sure Dad," she crooned and soothed him, held his hand in both hers until he had slipped off into sleep. Nothing more to do for him; she crept away from the bed, joined her mother and Gordon in the cafeteria, felt emptied, exhausted, ready to lean against the wall and sleep. She was glad when the doctor advised them to go home and get some rest before tomorrow when Joe was going to need them more. She was glad when after the long ride, pressed between her mother's hard cloth shoulder and Gordon's plump jacket, her .thigh constantly falling against his, glad when at the end she lurched into the warm house. There were no apples in the bowl. She dropped her clothes on the floor by her own bed without putting the lights on, fell into sleep in her own bed in her panties and bra, into a dreamless oblivion until the phone shrilled the Moynahan three rings to cut her from sleep into the bacon smell of Dinah's morning.

She hugged her pillow in the lovely warm of her own bed. Luxury. Her mother talking on the phone. The lavender wall pretty against the white paint of the drawers her father had stripped and painted up for her when she was ten. Her father. She turned to the door to listen to her mother talking on the phone, saw two shirts on hangers on the hook behind the lavender door, a shiny purple one with gathered sleeves, and a red plaid workshirt. Not her father's. Never. She sat up. Over by the closet door a pair of polished cowboy boots. So! They had let Gordon use her room. Her own room. Him!

"Angela darling, can I come in?" Her mother had tapped on the door and come in, an apron over her beige dress, carrying coffee. She looked tired.

"Mother," she said crossly to hurt, "you let Gordon use my room!" She pulled the lavender sheet up under her arms and took the coffee ungraciously. "Mother!" she scolded.

Dinah sat on the bed and sighed. "Drink your coffee," she said. "There's sugar in it. Darling, I have bad news."

Angela held the hot mug hard in her hands.

"Dad?" she said.

Her Mum nodded. "Sorry darling, he died in his sleep. I'm sorry."

"Are you. Are you." The wail came out of her belly and she closed her eyes not bearing to look at her mother.

It was all very well for her mother!

Oh, she could hear her mother treating her as though she were an edgy adolescent to be humoured, tentatively. "He would have wanted it, darling. Remember how he was about Rory's funeral. Everything had to be just right. That's what he paid life insurance for—final dignity."

Angela looked tiredly across the yellow table and knew her mother was right. Of course. Joe Moynahan would have wanted his widow and his daughter to be the best-dressed women there, at his funeral; his final dignity. Her poor Dad. The blue wall was heavy grey. Snow snaggled in unsteady wispings, trying to take hold across the colour-drained land.

"You really do have to come to Calgary with us, darling, and get a black outfit," Dinah humoured her. "Gordon will be here in half an hour."

Angela exploded. "Gordon! Gordon! I'm sick to death of relying on Gordon. Why didn't I get my driver's licence? It's the first thing I'm going to do after—all this. I can't understand you, Mother, that you never took the trouble," she ended mumbling, looking defeatedly out into the grey morning.

"Oh Angela, Angela. You really are uncharitable. Poor Gordon! He'd do anything for you, and I don't know what we should have done without him during the last few weeks. He means well, darling."

Angela snorted, "I suppose I could always marry him—then we could have him here for keeps making himself useful!"

"Oh don't be so silly, Angela. I know you're tired and upset —but—"

"Oh all right. I don't really have any choice, do I?" She dragged herself to her room to get ready to go to Calgary, looked with longing at her unmade bed. If she could just crawl back into it and sleep forever!

She dragged through the day; the long gravel-noisy drive,

lurching between Gordon and her mother; time at the funeral parlour with her mother calmly making the final arrangements for the lavish casket to be brought to the little church in Gladden. Angela waited, leaned against walls waiting, watching. Her mother was changed, more definite, crisper, less patient. Sometimes during the trying on of coats and boots and silly hats, Angela had a feeling that her mother would have liked to shake her, right there with Gordon watching, him, standing watching with his bulky blue jacket hanging open giving him lumbering size. Faithful ox, she kept thinking crossly.

Anyhow, she got a coat that was nipped in hard at the waist, very slim, just to dispel any doubts the Ellises had spread around. She would have liked grey trimming but her mother was firm, she had to have black fur at the neck and the cuffs and flaring at the bottom. The hat made her look pale, like the water-colour sketch with the Clara Jonason eyes still in her suitcase. She wasn't unpacked. She couldn't come home.

She felt pale at the funeral and kept her gloves on in the church while the neighbours filed by the casket to view her father all polished up by the funeral artists for the final inspection. "That's pagan. It's ghoulish," she had shouted at her mother just before Damion's parents drove up in the Chrysler to take them to church. Funny, in her absence, how something had grown up between her mother and the Goods. It wouldn't be her father. He couldn't stand them, them and their money!

Dinah was emphatic. "He has the funeral he would have wanted," she said. She was pale too, and somehow forbidding in her new black leather coat and a brimmed cloche that hid most of her hair. "Don't you understand anything about your father?" she snapped, seeing the unrelenting disapproval on her daughter's face. She frowned impatiently. She never used to use mascara, Angela thought critically, noticing the brown uptilt of her mother's lashes, then she heard herself shout like she'd shouted at her grandmother, sleazy spite filling the kitchen. "You might be surprised if you knew what I know about my father." She raised her hand to protect her face from the blow she expected to follow the fury of her mother's glance. But it never came.

"Pull yourself together. Here are the Goods," was all her

mother said—with ice. Then her mother never looked at her during the car ride. It still smelled leathery new, like it had when Damion had driven her in it. Mrs. Good tried to make conversation, said they'd just got a note from Damion saying he couldn't be home for Christmas. He'd got a chance to go with the firm he was working for to the north of Sweden. She was glad he was taking it. "You're only young once," she smiled, looked at Angela's pale face, then was quiet.

Her mother never looked at her during the church service. She let Gordon stand between them on the plastic green of the false grass at the graveside. It was cold. He was shivering in his thin dark suit without his blue jacket. No trees. Bare winter-bleached land stretched forever, pulled thin to the bottom of the impervious grey sky, death-white grey, weighing the land down to a thin beaten strip. Heavy snowflakes petalled down, slow motion, onto the mahogany lustre of the casket. Angela watched the pattern of each flake, watched snow petals turn to ghosts, blur away. She tried not to think of her brother down there, suffocated in the earth dark. She wanted to scream, rage for the boy, her brother down there with the smile on his face. She lifted her chin to pull her mind away from the hole, the grave, ruthless chasm, and she looked straight across it into the wise, watching eyes of Mrs. Ellis. Mrs. Ellis next to Mr. Ellis with a black band on the same white coat he had worn then under the street light, black band on the arm for her father, and the eyes measuring her across the snowflakes, same as they had through the steam with Silvia humming. Her mind fell into its own chasm and she felt her knees go weak, reached out and caught at the nearest arm. Gordon's. She pulled herself together. But Gordon supported her arm and gradually, as the priest's words fell down onto her father with damp sods of loose earth, he put her gloved hand between his two large bare ones, his warmth going through to her fingers, and he stood in very close to her side, kept hold of her arm as the mourners dispersed across the mud between the few snow-gathering tombstones.

"Don't you bother about the chores tonight," he said as she got back into the Chrysler. "I'll be around and see to everything."

And he was.

Angela, with nothing but irritability between herself and her mother, the place not seeming like home, had pleaded tired and gone to her room. While she had been away, they had established a routine without her. She couldn't fit into the pattern yet. She wasn't part of it here.

At least she could finish unpacking her luggage. Perhaps then she would feel she had come home. The mess. She could see it now the funeral was over, the activity ended. Bed unmade. Brown case open, spilling over. The flight bag spread out against the wall. She fell onto the crumpled bed and buried her face in the pillows, then got up to pull the curtains over the window, close out the faces of the night with her little-girl curtains her mother had covered with designs of delicate bold thistledown and blue butterflies. Then she pulled the bed straight and tried to rest on it, bent the neck of the table lamp to point the light down. But behind her eyes the graveyard kept coming back and her brother smiling through blackness, and the Ellises looking knowingly across the snows. My poor Dad! My mother is in the kitchen writing letters so she won't have to think. And I shall clear up my room.

She hung up the crushed clothes from the flight bag, shook out the dress she had worn on her flight away to England, when a middle-aged woman had told her she was quite beautiful. Long time ago. Before . . . Under the dress, under the shoes, two elastic panty-girdles, always hidden from when Grandmother might have snooped and found them. Now she put them, like souvenirs, in the bottom drawer with her childhood treasures; old exercise books with pressed flowers between the pages, and school photographs, outgrown pretty clothes she couldn't bear to throw away; in the bottom drawer of the chest her father had enamelled white and dressed up with twirly silver handles, the summer when she was ten.

At the bottom of the shoe compartment, in the dust from the shoes, dust of London, the bakery, Clara's yard, the back alleys, and home, three worn green exercise books—journal of summer —the continuing assignment. Together with exercise book four and *Women Poets of Canada* she put them in the circle of light on her bedside table. Her mother's sketches from the old brown suitcase she put in the bottom drawer with the things she had to keep—but out of sight.

When the last things were put away she stood on her white

enamelled chair to lift the brown suitcase and the flight bag onto the top high shelf of her closet. Summer over. Journey finished. Lock it away—all except the exercise books.

She sat in the mauve pillows with night closed out behind the little-girl thistledown curtains and tried to write in a clean section of exercise book four. She didn't even want to see, not catch a glimpse of the pages that went before—not yet. Perhaps never. Pretend it never happened. Run away. Always run away. Let everybody down. Mr. Olson thinks that making words for the thoughts is her way of surviving, like my mother has used the materials of our poor life to sew out feelings, and somewhere another father makes music. But, I let everybody down. Why should you be any different? You with your mocking eyes prodding. I suppose you think I owe it to you to survive, Mr. Olson.

I do not dare to close my eyes. It is December and I am full of graveyards tossing, and weary. Track eight is splitting in my head and hacking the backs of my eyes, filling them with splinters of broken film. Reach out the hands to ease the eyes, arms to cradle my father, little shrunken man. Split the eyes into a graveyard with snow falling. Remember the turn of the feet in new expensive tall boots, turning away, walking away without looking back, leaving you there. Alone. Cruel last cut through the umbilical cord—to turn and leave him there, alone with the humped little tombstones. Oh Dad. There was nothing else to do but turn around and leave you. Then, when we weren't looking, they would roll up the plastic green and leave you. Alone. Crying against the wind outside the lonely flat edge of town. Crying. Lying. But people can't lie on their deathbeds. You said it wasn't true. But there are stretchmarks on my belly. Will they ever go? Because it isn't true. My father said he knew it wasn't true. A baby upside down in my eyes arches its back and looks round at me with my father's face, without his teeth, his eyes pleading. Oh cradle my little father, cradle him for ever in my words, in my pages. My poor Dad.

I must get my driver's licence now I am home.

I am home now the room is tidy and summer packed away. And free. Almost. If. Would Damion have come home for Christmas if he had known I was going to be here?

In the days after the funeral Angela wondered why she was staying home. She was free and she had money. Her days a limbo, weary, hung vague with purposeless hours while her mother worked on calmly. One long afternoon, Dinah said that really there was no point in keeping the farm now, did Angela think? For her own part she would rather be in a big centre where she could advance her work technically and build a market. And Angela would be going away to university next year, anyway, wouldn't she? "Land prices are very high," she said. "Really, we are very well provided for." With her head on one side Dinah talked calmly, watching her fingers snipping loops of golden yarn in the spiky pattern of her new tapestry.

Angela leaned across the bowl of sprouting bulbs on the wide ledge and pressed her forehead to the cold window, saw snow mounting thick on the wind-break of the evergreens, snow falling featherly, steadily, tying white sky to white land with flimsy garlands. She breathed out making a cloud on the window, closed her snow-dizzied eyes, tired. "I suppose," she said dully, not contradicting, not wanting to face up to what her mother was saying, the leaving, but knowing grudgingly that her mother had already left, given up on the farm. Her mother! Her mother was whirling away in her own orbit somewhere, singing somewhere, you could tell by the way the scissors snipped definitively and by some withheld force in the voice, a holding back of happiness. Happiness not decent so soon, yet.

"I have applied for a Canada Council grant to do a year's intensive study."

Angela didn't want to answer. How callous. That application must have been made before her father was sick. She frowned, defeated, and saw sad comedy in the puffed snow caps inching taller on the fencepost tops. "Good fences make good neighbours," her Dad had said and nodded his head sagely, wise expression to make up for his lack of education, always the heavy pretence of wisdom. Oh Dad. Poor Dad. "Five strands make a better job of it than three," advice given like a confidence out of sombre eyes. Oh Dad. She laughed. She didn't know why. "We dug all those post holes by hand," she said. "It took half a lifetime to get all the fences done. My father's lifetime."

"But they got done. Didn't they?" Dinah was offhand. Her scissors made a longer crunching snip infuriating the eyes at the window.

Angela laughed again, laughed to hurt, to pull her mother into her own pain. "I never knew how Rory could stand there so trusting, holding the post while Dad swung at it, pounded it down. Rory had such faith in Dad." She closed her eyes on the memory of her Dad balanced precariously on an upturned oil drum and Rory looking up at him laughing. She laughed again.

Dinah looked up momentarily at her daughter watching the snow. "If I get the grant, and I think I will . . ." She paused.

"Such miles of fences to have put in by hand, in the heat. The wind."

"Well, we're lucky the place is in such good shape now, aren't we? And the whole place is in very good shape," her English accent had become more pronounced. "All these things will help us get a good price for the place."

Angela said nothing, pressed her forehead and her nose to the window like a child. Snow like blossoms weighing on the arms of the evergreens. Why had her mother planted the trees and tended them through all their little years if now she could leave them so easily? No birds. No life. Snow growing, erasing the fields and the reality, blossoms on the evergreens, heavy blossoms. Her legs felt weak and her breath trembled onto the window. She leaned her hands heavily on the ledge. Now her father was dead it was like life hemorrhaging away, like in hospital with blood on her feet, everything floating away, close the eyes, all the summers, all the harvests and the oil-smelling roar of the tractor, gulls screaming. And her horse. What would become of Ami? And what would become of Rory's horse? She scrubbed at the cloud of her breath on the window. Rubbed it away with the side of her hand. Her Mother. Oh Dad.

"If I do get the grant, it will be for use in England, at the London Institute of Technology."

Her mother. Unable to disguise the excitement in her. Not even subtle.

Snap.

"I suppose you can't wait to get going and find Jeffrey Jonason." Her voice trembled at the audacity of her words.

The scissors stopped snipping. Snow dropped; a curtain. Silence forever falling, falling.

Then.

"Do you have to be so childish?" Her mother's voice was impatient. "What are you expecting me to say to such childishness?"

Snow falling. Heavy flakes. Heavy silence.

"Really Angela! Do you think it likely that you would run back to Damion Good after twenty years? Really! How childishly romantic can you get?"

Yes. Yes. I would. She felt her own ache strident under her mother's scathing. How nice to have somebody to run to! She didn't dare move now she had said the name, given words to the thought about Jeffrey Jonason, but she shrugged to imply that she couldn't care less. She meant to keep her cool; then she heard herself shouting. "Sure Dad's farm will fetch a good price. I am quite sure you can sell my Dad's work for a very good price. His life's work. Poor Dad."

"Angela." Dinah's voice firm, very controlled. "Be realistic. It happens. We're not the only ones. Even Goods expect to sell out in a few years. Damion doesn't think he will want to farm."

"Oh, he wouldn't," her reaction welled out nastily. "But my poor Dad, that's different. Always unlucky. Cheated. You cheated him. But sure, sure he left us well provided for." Venom came out with the words, and she braced her shoulders angrily to withstand her mother. Her own violence was making her tremble. She held on to the ledge. One of them had left the tap dripping in that blue bathroom. Drip. Drip. Drip, into the quakes of her breathing.

"Angela."

Angela is a fierce name said like that, like the knife across a pig's throat when her father was butchering. Head pulled up, blood—

"Angela, will you turn round and look at me." It was a command. Steel-edged.

She turned round but tossed her head and sucked in her cheeks to show she couldn't care less, returned the cut of the look, hard. Dinah still sat on her legs in the corner of the flowered chesterfield under the blue wall now bare of its tapestry of rioting angels. She had put her new work down across the table, a procession of porcupines like a golden army advancing in sunshine across red leaves. She looked at Angela direct, controlled, unsmiling.

"Get this one thing straight, my dear, once and for all. I never cheated Joe Moynahan, any more than he ever cheated you . . ." she paused and frowned, added, "knowingly." She said the words slowly giving each its cold emphasis. This wasn't the old, gentle, vague Dinah. This was a Clara Jonason. A fierce woman. "Just remember, he chose to have you as his daughter as he chose to have me as his wife. Without melo-drama," she added critically, raising an eyebrow, blade across the throat and a shudder inside. Blood again, letting life away.

"You mean he knew? All the time?" Her chest was gasping and her words trembled. "He gave me . . ."

"He knew. Of course he knew."

She shouted again, shouted to shake the windows. "And you want us to sell his farm? He loved this place. It's all that's left of him and you want to sell it." Her voice steadied to raging iciness. "You kill me!" she finished and flaunted from the sun-porch to the kitchen, picked up the phone. She asked Gordon if she drove to his place in their truck if he would come with her into Gladden to do her driver's test. "They say they can fit me in," she told him shortly.

She closed her mind off to home and her mother, focussed it on a dead blankness, drove, and passed her test. Hard, dead blankness. This was her town, small town. These were her people. Her mother may run away but—Angela and Gordon went into the pool hall after her test to stand around and drink Coke, exchange gossip with the guys and a couple of girls from her grade twelve who hadn't left. "You sure are skinny, Ange,"

Leona Murray kept saying and pulling her jacket across her own new pregnancy. "Bill and me didn't mean to have a kid yet—but what the heck—it's happened."

"Bet it's real good to get back to Canada," everybody kept saying and asked what they were going to do with the farm now poor old Joe had passed on.

Before they left Gladden, she bought a big plastic bag of red apples and put them on the seat between herself and Gordon. She drove. "I can't think why I didn't get my licence before," she said. "I've been driving this thing since before I could reach the pedals."

"I guess you always had me around to drive, remember Ange?" Gordon patted her thigh and leaned towards her across the apples. "Eh Ange, you don't think Dinah'll sell your place, do you?"

"No. I'm sure she won't," she said and accelerated through the rutted brown snow of the road. "And Gordon, don't smoke in my truck, eh. I hate the smell of cigarettes."

"Okay Ange," he said, looking at her with surprise in his baby-blue eyes. "Okay Ange. Anything you say." He put his pack of Rothmans back in his top pocket.

"Are you mad at me about something, Ange?" he asked her as she turned in at his gate towards the bare house at the top of the straight stem of a road, like a house in a child's drawing. She pulled up alongside his '59 G.M. by the door.

"No," she said and looked down at him as he stood in the broken snow by his unpainted doorway looking worriedly up at her before he closed the truck door. She smiled at him. "No, of course I'm not mad at you, Gordon. Why should I be?" You have to learn not to be mad at anybody, cool, like her mother, her mother who would have the coffee on when she got home and would treat her carefully as though she were merely adolescent, touchy.

And that's the way it was. Dinah convivial, speaking reasonably, "You know, darling, we don't have to sell if you feel so strongly about it. It just seemed the reasonable thing to do, to me. The most sensible."

Her mother! Angela shrugged, tipped the red apples into the wide empty bowl, deliberately, flauntingly walked over to put the plastic bag in the garbage under the sink, came back and deliberately polished the red apples with a blue-edged tea-towel. "It's not home without apples in the bowl," she said curtly.

"We could rent it out—or come to some sort of arrangement with somebody."

Angela rubbed the yellow table with the cloth, closing her mother out.

"I know I don't want to live here now. You will be away at university—that covers several years."

"I got my driver's licence."

"Oh good."

"I'm driving into Calgary tomorrow. I have enough money. I'm going to buy a typewriter." She neither looked at her mother nor with the voice invited any sharing of interest. She wanted to close her out, punish her.

"Is anyone going with you?"

"No," she said with finality.

"Darling, the roads are bad. I do hope you won't have trouble with the truck."

"If I do, I'll cope. Don't worry. And I shall do the chores now and I shall do the chores before I go in the morning and I shall be home in time to do the chores tomorrow." She was cold, belligerent, emphatic.

"But darling, you really don't have to work yourself so. You don't have to get up to do the chores. Gordon can come over. He needs the work and you're probably hurting his feelings by not getting his help."

"Oh Poor Gordon! I bleed for him. And for us poor things who haven't got enough about us to care for my father's place." Scorn serrated her words and she looked through Dinah to the brilliance of the half-worked tapestry hung across the back of her father's worn chair. "It might be nice for us, the Moyna-hans, to be self-sufficient for once." Then she thought better of it and added, "But don't worry, I'll get Gordon if we really need him—ever."

That night she sat in her father's chair while her mother worked with her porcupine autumn-glowing tapestry all over the kitchen table. They kept the television on to disguise the chasm between them, and half watching it, Angela doodled on clean pages in her diary, exercise book four. She doodled round the edges of a page, then turned the doodles into a corral of fenceposts joined together with five strands of barbed scribbled tangles. She watched her mother and her work reflected in the television screen comedy and wrote with the emptiness of one who had dodged the impact of the day and only seen the events scribbled on the calendar.

Today I got my driver's licence. Tomorrow I am going to Calgary, alone. I hate my mother. A month ago tonight I went into hospital. Tomorrow I am getting a typewriter. A gadget. All tracks switched off. Numb. Nothing. Dull. Slow. Empty. But I will pay off my debts, Mr. Olson. Your assignments typed neatly with perfect margins. If I pay off all the debts, then I will close my eyes without track eight blinding. If I pay the debts perhaps then track eight will let my mind go free. My mother thinks she has paid her debts. My Mother.

It was all so easy when you could drive yourself, careen in your own orbit, free orbit, yourself at the wheel, exhilarating the long snow-rutted slippery miles, coping. But there are limitations to recklessness, and she drove into the first large shopping mall on the nearest edge of the city, not wanting to tempt fate too far by pressing the old truck through the intricacies of inner city traffic. Next time.

How funny; it was Christmas in the stores and she had forgotten because Christmas wasn't the right mood for home this year. No child. Close out the baby. No love to spare.

First she found a clinic, a medical complex with a whole spate of doctors. No trouble. She got her post-natal check-up and asked for a prescription for a year's supply of contraceptive pills, the whole year, because she lived so far out of town. She bought the whole supply at the adjoining drug store. "I am planning to get married," she had explained to an impersonal doctor. No hassles. Easy world when your mind is hard. Practical. Numb. And you have your own money.

She bought an electric typewriter with the eight weeks' hoarded wages from Tunnicliffe's bakery, two hundred and fifty-eight dollars, and two five-hundred-sheet boxes of manuscript typing paper. She began to feel like her mother, singing somewhere, raring to get home and get started, to touch the keys.

Back home, as soon as the chores were done, she set herself up on the kitchen table to get in tune with her typewriter and pay off the first of the bills. Dinah sat on the arm of her father's old chair with the tapestry, stitch by stitch, gathering flame across her knees.

Pay off the little bills first, double-spaced, quick, with perfect margins. One merrily written off to the Tunnicliffes to thank them for all they had done, to tell them that since her father's death had cut short her travels and made it essential for her to

162

stay home to look after the farm, she had invested her earnings from them in the typewriter she was now using. She expected that it was settled for her that she would have to turn her career towards writing since that would fit in with the farm.

She wrote with sunshine to Mike Tupp, and said unashamedly how lucky she had been to have him take such good care of her. But now she had to settle down, keep her father's farm going, because there was no one else to take care of it. Remember her brother had been drowned. I just may have to marry a farmer and live happily ever after, she joked and wished him a Merry Christmas.

She wrote a special gentle Christmas letter for Madeleine, yellow-skinned Madeleine who had kept watch on the landing outside the bathroom, Madeleine with the knowing eyes. Perhaps she was dead already. How vile to have been glad that the poor old thing had been taken away to hospital, off the landing, just to make it easier in Angela Moynahan's mind. Now, Angela wrote of the soft snow, and the green scent of summer in the heart of stiff yellow bales, and cows' breath in the cold morning, and the sadness of the little farm now her father was not here. She addressed the long airmail envelope with a "please forward" just in case. Poor Madeleine.

To Clara Jonason it was not easy to write. "I am glad I met you. I feel certain that my mother will be renewing her—" she didn't know what word to use. She crumpled the page and began again. "My mother's work is growing, is very intense, and I feel certain she will be in England soon. At present I am not certain what I shall be doing, except that, like my mother's thing is art, so mine is writing. So I shall be writing—something —but the pages will never look so good on the walls as did my mother's work. When you know who you are your choices are made quite clear, don't you think?" She ended with a question, half hoping as she typed that Clara would answer.

How to write to the grandparents? Not easy. She thanked them and thanked them again for all they had given her, said that next time she went to town she was going to look for an English rubber hot-water bottle. It had been so nice to have. She told them about the driver's licence and the ride through the snow to Calgary, and the typewriter, and the work her mother was doing. She ended with a row of kisses in blue ball-point, the way her father might have done. Happy Christmas and a thousand kisses. Then she sealed the envelope quickly, before she could change her mind. It was costing her nothing to be phony, was it?

"Your fingers are flying," Dinah said, looking up and smiling.

"I've really got the hang of it," she smiled back forgetting her hostility in the exhilaration of getting her own thing done. "I think I'll just write a note to Damion, for Christmas; then would you like me to make coffee?"

A frivolous note full of wisecracks to be easy, saying she had told him the North would hook him, note to Damion, not really caring tonight with the type keys flying and her mind absorbed and singing.

With coffee, they took the porcupine tapestry into the other room and hung it on the blue wall for Dinah to see how it was coming. Porcupines, spiky, catching the sunglow, an excitement of texture.

"You know, it's not home without your things on the walls," Angela conceded. Her mother just laughed and smiled at the new hanging with her head on one side.

"I have someone I have to send a piece of your work to. Would you mind if I took my peacock shoulder bag apart? I want to send one side to an American I met, from Montana."

She emptied the contents from it onto her bed and Dinah herself unpicked the joins, cleaned and pressed the two sides. Then they packed one side in tissue between two cards, wrapped it carefully with a note that said she had had to come home because of her father's death, and ended, "between travellers passing". Angela addressed the parcel to Sam Lubinkoff, care of his family on a rural route out of a small town in Montana.

The other half of the peacock bag she fastened onto a space of lavender wall in her bedroom and underneath set the old red card-table that had been folded up under the hanging coats and coveralls behind the white drawers and plant screen for as long as she could remember.

"I'm going to work in my room, Mum," she explained. "I kept a journal of my travels and I think I'm going to write it up, fill it out, make a sort of book."

"How nice; what a good idea," Dinah encouraged and brought a cloth and a can of wax to clean up the old table.

Businesslike and enthusiastic, the hostility gone, Angela and Dinah set up the place for working, the typewriter plugged in with a long extension cord, box of manuscript paper ready, four green exercise books and a box under the table for the discarded pages. Dinah put a blue cushion on the white painted chair and brought in an extra lamp not needed in her bedroom now Joe was dead. Then her mother sat on the bed and Angela sat at the card-table work-table, sipping their coffee. At last I have come home, Angela thought, and typed a page like her diary before she went to sleep.

I have to do this thing. Set it straight. Remember your mocking eyes, Mr. Olson, that dared us all to be honest, to dare to commit to words such things as quiver inside, where to be secure is to face the quivering and the uncertainty. You gave me a debt every time you wrote "Excellent" in the margin. Oh, don't mock, I shall pay the debts. If I don't do it, one night I shall close my eyes and the baby they called Angelina will arch her back and look at me with your eyes turned sad, another murder, my murder, your murder, death of everything, no survival.

While Dinah worked steadily on the massive tapestry and kept the calm of the house, Angela did the chores, and when they were done immersed herself in her writing, writing for atonement.

Christmas, the world itself, all got closed out of the farmhouse; they were periphery things, mere interruptions to the involvement of creating. Days went by into January with no further mention of selling the place; days of oasis, snow-soft peace, two women working, their eyes closed against seeding and harvest, closed against the end of a tapestry, against the end of a journal of summer. Time hanging tranquil.

In the middle of January the weather turned very cold, freezing her breath and her eyelashes as she went about the chores. It was getting time to think about loading a bunch of pigs for auction. Some mornings after the chores were done, the necessary, real things, she looked at the first page of the day in her typewriter and she doubted. Was she taking time in self-indulgent, story-weaving girl stuff? Sometimes she looked with satisfaction through the immaculate completed pages, put them in the lid of the typing-paper box and tested the weight of them in her hands. Even the weight of the typed pages was sometimes impressive, exciting, now she was out of exercise book one and past one hundred. Getting it out, spelling it out in a story, the watcher watching the tracks of the mind unwind, telling the unwinding. But was it just a girl stuff? Useless? She wondered, would it be good enough for Mr. Olson to put check marks down the side of the page and sometimes an "Excellent" at the bottom? Or would he think it was bad, maudlin? She couldn't tell. Twice, two days, she lost faith altogether in the worth of the telling and went out to do valuable things, shovelled out the barns, dug out pathways through the snow, ploughed out the driveway with the blade on the front of the tractor. Gordon drove up the freshly ploughed-out driveway and said she didn't have to do such things, she ought to know that he would come round and do the heavy jobs. But he was too late; she worked like mad so she had everything done and they had no need to call him. It was satisfying when the farm work was done; she knew it was well done. She could measure it. But the writing was different.

"I miss Mr. Olson," she said to her mother, out of all context, in one of those spells when she couldn't convince herself to get on with her writing and was making herself another sandwich to occupy time. Not that she would have shown her personal struggle to organize her experience into literary form to Mr. Olson. No. She was only thinking how different it is to keep up with assignments when there are check marks down the side of a page and sometimes an "Excellent" for confirmation of worth.

"You were lucky to have him all through high school," Dinah made small talk, gossip, like a casual observer. "He lasted very well, a man of his calibre, for this community."

Her mother. As though she wasn't part of this community. Angela looked at her and felt anger. "You mean they petitioned him out," she said and knew she was right. It had happened before, so many times, the petitioning out of free thinkers, on some little excuse, like they didn't fit the community values. "Did you try to stop it?"

"Of course," her mother raised her hands palms up and shrugged, then put out coffee mugs. "He was offered a transfer to another school, but he didn't take it."

"No. He's travelling in Europe. He wrote to me." Angela spoke coldly and glowered at her mother, question and anger in the glance that blamed. "My people! My ignorant people" her voice shook with loathing.

Dinah shrugged as though it was no business of hers and Angela stood up infuriated. Her mother. She'd already left, hadn't she! Took no responsibility. "Oh," Dinah said calmly, throwing it off casually without turning to look at her daughter, "It's just that they suspect excellence. They mistake it for worldly evil." They!

Angela looked hard at her mother's back and remembered Sam the American. "It's fear of innocence," he had said, and a London back street came vivid into her mother's kitchen, run round a lamp-post into exhilaration. Sam the American and her mother would understand each other. They could both run away! "Some things make me mad," was all she said and tossed her head and went back to her typewriter determined to the pages because of the covenant she had with herself to survive, because of the debt Mr. Olson had given her. Write. Write and sting out the wounds. Out of the scars pull butterfly words. Remember a drab green classroom and a bird crying at the bars, and the eyes mocking, always mocking, daring you to come alive.

Mr. Olson I am trying to be born, to take hold.

She stayed up half the night trying to type into the web of her story the fears of her people, to clarify, to explain their rejection of any but the ones who speak in their own voices, tried to explain their fear of a vagrant idea. She crumpled a lot of pages, dissatisfied. It was so difficult because her people would have put up with her teacher if they could only have been sorry for him; if his house had burned down, or his debts piled up, or his daughter got pregnant. Then he would have been one of "us". It was free-winging ideas they had to petition out democratically. Murder. She couldn't sort it out—the strange arrogance of her people. She got frustrated with the writing because she couldn't make it work. She went to bed angry at it and her mother and the stupid community, woke up unrefreshed not wanting to get up and go out to the chores in the half-light morning, but she made herself.

It was cold. Her finger ends froze through her gloves as she forked out clumps of stiff bales for the cows and her legs quivered inside her jeans. Why hadn't she layered herself with panty-hose? She pulled her parka hood forward over her face and pushed her chin down into the fur and walked across the wind to empty a bucket of oats across the fence for the horses. Then suddenly she was guilty. Their yesterday's ration was still cupped in the ice crust of snow where she had left it. They always came to the fence. She had known yesterday when they weren't there that she should have investigated. But she had been too concerned about getting back in to her writing. Now, she called, "Ami, Ami, Prince," but her voice was nothing in the sift of the wind. She got under the wire and walked across the flat half-white calling against the blowing snow. Silly, she thought, walking out to look for horses, silly woman thing. But her father would never have neglected to look for them. Her brother's horse.

She followed the old tracks, iced and uneven in the deep snow. Hard to walk on. Her thighs were freezing through the icing cloth of her jeans when she smelled the horse smell and found them behind the leaning boards of the old pioneer cabin her father could never bear to pull down. Her horse whinnied and she leaned against him, put her arms round his neck and leaned into the rough warmth of his ice-crystalled mane; like rest, refuge, out of the wind. When she'd caught her breath she felt sorry for leaving her brother's horse out of the fussing. "Hi Prince," she whispered and reached over to touch his face, but his ears went back, he shuddered, bared his teeth and pulled away.

Then she saw blood on the trampled snow and inched with her back to the boards of the cabin to look for the wound. She saw it; held her iced gloved hand over her mouth. The chest was blown open, a hole oozing like liver, blood icicles slivering down his legs. Somebody had shot him. She couldn't get near him; he quivered and shied away. She tried leading her horse away by the mane while coaxing her brother's horse to follow out into the wind. Twice she walked a hundred yards slowly, twice she went back for him. She had to get him, her brother's horse, into the barn but every time she approached him he flung his hind quarters round at her and warned her off. It was no good. Gasping into the wind with her nose running and her eyes weeping of cold and the fur of her parka wet to her chin, she stumbled back across the ice-humped tracks to the phone.

"Gordon, should I get the vet?" She sounded as though she was crying, but it was the cold.

"Hold on," he said. "I'll be right there. Pick up bridles and blankets for both of them. I'll look to everything else."

"You'll get pneumonia," her mother said and made her take time to put on extra clothes. Her mother. So calm. But she didn't care.

Then she and Gordon were puffing together against the wind, wordless, hurrying.

"Fucking hunters," he said and moved gently round the flinching horse, wheedling him, coaxing him. "My lovely, my beauty," working his hands nearer, until he was fondling the cheeks, pushing the ice from around the eyes, coaxing, soothing. He slipped the bridle on, coaxing, speaking love words all the time.

Angela turned away, choked up, bridled her own horse, brushed off his back, watching, listening.

Gordon went on coaxing, the voice of endearment, "Come

and hold his head, Ange, hold him steady, my lovely. I'll get a shot of penicillin into him now, the sooner the better, eh my lovely? Hold still, my beauty. There's my beauty."

She rode Ami slowly back to the barn while Gordon led the other, her brother's horse, talking him in, coaxing, loving. Then she watched while Gordon backed the frightened horse into a narrow stall, coaxing, loving, kept him on his feet and cleaned the mess of the wound, dried the horse down, kept him blanketed, talked to him, fondled him with gentle hands, baby-talked him, cradled him in the sweet hay-scented warmth. When the quivering stopped and the horse breathed evenly, Angela sat down on the straw heap in the corner and shook, her teeth chattering out of control.

"You're cold, Ange." He sat down and put his arms round her, pulled her into the thickness of his padded jacket. "He's going to be okay, I think. But I don't want to leave him just yet. Want to keep an eye on him just in case," he said and pushed her parka hood back and stroked her hair, soothing her shivering. "Don't worry, my lovely, my beauty," he crooned. "He'll be all right now," he rubbed her icy thighs. "Don't you worry about a thing, we'll take good care of our Rory's Prince."

Her brother's horse would be all right now. Gordon knew about these things. She leaned against him, let herself be warmed, soothed, taken care of.

Home free, if she just relaxed. Warm.

He would never have murdered his child.

Okay, marry him. Pay all the debts. What the heck! Why was she fighting? It's what her Dad would have wanted her to do, be a good girl, settle down. But she couldn't stop shivering. The cold had gone to her and she had to go to bed, stayed there for three days with a temperature and without a voice, feeling again that life was slipping away while she hugged her mauve pillow and kept her eyes closed, willed herself down into warmth and sleep away from the concern of her mother. Close out the wind at the window and the roar of the '59 truck coming and leaving, and close out the voices of Gordon and her mother polite in the kitchen.

She had said she would marry him, had she? It would be so easy. Be a good girl. Settle down. Just lie in bed and dream the next pages, the next chapter, dream it real, wherever real is. Somebody else is doing the chores. She is free.

"Darling, you can't be serious," her mother sat on the bed on the fourth morning. Her mother. So immaculate and considerately polite. But she was serious. Wasn't it all working out for the best, working out fine? Fate. Exactly right. A letter from England came to say that Grandmother Dawson had to go into hospital the first week of March for an operation. It was only decent that Dinah should be there. It all fit in fine as though it were intended. If she married him in Calgary on February twenty-seventh, then they could see her mother off at the airport right after the ceremony. No. No. No. No churches, no dress. No. No celebration.

Everything was working out. The grant had come through and Dinah would be starting her course at the Institute of Technology in London after Easter. And she would never come back to live in Gladden. Angela knew that. Her mother was going home. She was home free. Singing.

Oh Dad. My poor Dad. She's rubbed you out. She!

Once, only once, Dinah frowned and said she would like to shake Angela. Strong words from her. Angela turned her head to look at the expression, light blue eyes puzzled, troubled, like the dark blue eyes of the young doctor who had shaken her, actually shaken her. "Get with it, woman," he had said. Blood on her pale thin feet. But that had been different. He had thought she was going to die.

"You don't understand, Mother," she said tiredly, trying to dismiss the whole thing and get back to her typewriter. She ignored her mother and her backache, her weariness, until she had written twenty pages right off to make up for lost days, pages the ghost of her summer, ghost life real of their own, absorbing, crawling out of the green exercise books onto immaculate pages of a growing novel, tape unwinding, snake-easing out to the gloomed tangle of her mind.

So let Gordon do the chores. What the heck!

She sat facing the wild peacock, from the half of her shoulder bag, hanging on the mauve wall, and she let herself be taken over by the girl called Angela who had kept a green journal; neat, neat pages; compact, controlled hysteria, staring from faint ruled lines with fierce white eyes. Who was Angela? Who is Angela? Write her out of the memory of the choking mind, make her a fiction. The woman at the typewriter is not the girl in the exercise books. The girl at the typewriter is the student forever doing the assignment, absorbed, happy to be lost in the problem of creation. The pages grow, a thing being born. Birth. Panting towards a settled form. Pick up the pages, hold the miracle of the weight of them in incredulous hands.

"Come back," her mother would say at meal times and snap her fingers against her daughter's nose. "You'll get lost in that thing you're writing."

"I intend to," she said, coldly intending to rub out her mother just as her mother had rubbed out her father, and she went back to the writing until there were three hundred and fifty-four pages and the story needed an ending.

February the seventeenth; the pages had to have an ending for the sake of artistic unity. February the seventeenth; the ladies of Gladden were putting on her bridal shower. February the seventeenth; the day for all the ends to tie in neatly.

It was not easy to compose the last pages.

She doodled on the typewriter like a student writing lines. "The end is the beginning," she typed twice on a line, twenty-five lines. Fifty affirmations.

The green exercise books had never ended, and the girl in the pages was left stranded in the girl at the typewriter who had to invent an ending she wanted. She invented it quickly, embarrassed because it was a fiction tagged on to the end of her truth. She fairy-taled that the story-book Angela let nothing be wasted and wrote a novel of her experiences that was the beginning of her habit of writing. Her apprenticeship. And she had the story-book girl dedicate the novel "to Angelina" because all debts should be paid for artistic unity.

Angela Moynahan, who was soon to become Mrs. Kopec, put the pages together in the typing-paper box that she'd emptied, taped the lid down very firmly and wrote on it with a wide red felt pen just SUMMER, then put the box in the corner of her white enamelled drawer under the other souvenirs that she couldn't throw away, but she put this one there with an exuberance of satisfaction. She had done it! Wow! Now, she

172

must find out how to get in touch with Mr. Olson and tell him she had made a beginning to work up to his expectation.

She ran out onto the roadway without a coat and slid like a kid on the icy patches, faster, faster. She threw snowballs with bare hands up into her mother's nurtured evergreens to bring down sifts and sifts of startled snowfalls. Then the '59 truck drove in and Gordon called from the cab that she'd better come in because there was some mail for her.

She laughed, she didn't know why, when he flopped the mail on the kitchen table. Artistic unity! There was a letter from New York from Sam Lubinkoff, Sam the American, saying that eventually he had got her gift and was hoping to see her again as he would be in the West in April on a concert tour. Just a little tour in small halls, "but a beginning" he wrote. She put his letter on her work table by the typewriter and wanted to write back right away because she felt like it. But she had to get ready for her bridal shower, feeling her mother's disapproval heavy in the house and in her extreme care with Gordon. Her mother. So she doesn't approve. So. So. So. It's all right for her; her debts are paid, she thinks. My poor old Dad. She doesn't care about rubbing you out. You were the kind one. Oh Dad!

The bridal shower was in the community hall that used to be the schoolhouse in the pioneer days of not so long ago. 1938 was still in black paint over the doors, double brown doors into the dark porch with pegs for the children's coats at the top of the worn stairs. She left her boots with the others in the pile at the bottom of the steps where the snow was melting from them into a pool of wet, slipping over down the basement steps in dark patches.

She loved the smell of the old school, wood-warm and oiled floors, the brownness cosy, now with a whiff of coffee because the ladies had come in early to get the urn going.

The big room was decorated with a few yellow and green streamers, but the windows were all boarded up now, the big old school windows, because one Hallowe'en a long time ago boys had put shots through them. Once a flustered pheasant had crashed in at the largest window and shattered the glass. When the people came for a meeting one of the men had to hit the pheasant with the back of a broken desk to finish it off before it broke another window trying to get out. So all the windows were boarded up now with brown sheets of board; dull background for the decorations saved from shower to shower, yellow and green streamers interwound, fanning out from the wire above the central lightbulb to make an arch over the teacher's oak desk, the altar to the bride, to all the brides of the district.

For Angela, the central decoration, her special emblem under the arch of streamers, was a magazine cut-out of two magnificent horses' heads, proud Arabians, because the ladies said, "Everybody knows, horses is the thing she's craziest about, next to Gordon." Everybody laughed and all the ladies covered her with smiles of welcome. She didn't know what to say. She was never any good with small talk. She looked around for somebody to talk to, but the girls from her class were busy slicing the cakes and lifting the pieces onto platters. She dumped her funeral coat on a desk just inside the door and twirled across to the cake cutters, swinging her hair. "Well, somebody sure seems happy," somebody laughed in a big accent. The girls went on lifting the cake slices. She felt like telling them she'd written a sort of book and that's why she was happy. But she didn't. She said how nice the cakes looked.

Mrs. Ellis pinned the corsage on to begin the ceremony, slipping her cold fingers inside the neck of Angela's fluffy blouse. Her hands smelled faintly of bleach. The corsage was a yellow rose half opened with a tight bud close against it, bedded in fern and tied up with a metallic silver ribbon. It tickled under her chin.

They played games she wasn't any good at, she with her brain! She didn't know the birthstone for November, nor the flower for March, nor the emblem of Nova Scotia. She couldn't even get the tail on the donkey any nearer than in its ear. But she picked up squiggles of news and gossip. Mrs. Ellis introduced her to the wife of the teacher who had come to take Mr. Olson's place. "He sure left a mess for my husband to take over," the wife said by way of friendly woman-to-womaness, "and he sure doesn't seem to have taught the kids much." "Oh," Angela looked down into the thinness of the bouffant sprayed hairdo and turned away to the little bingo they were organizing. She won the prize, a pair of oven mitts decorated with kittens' faces, and she said that was what she's always wanted. Weren't they lovely?

Somebody was saying they couldn't be too sure about keeping the new Anglican minister yet. He'd preached against work on Sunday. He didn't seem the right man for a farm community.

The ribbon was getting scratchier under her chin and when she bent her head the slight scent from the opening rose distracted her, haunting. Yellow rose she had written into her book and given to Mr. Isseppi, yellow rose cradled in white wrapping, spilling scent in London grey. She kept smiling to remember the pages completed. Everybody said she looked lovely; the thought of marriage must be suiting her. Such a good boy, Gordon. Her father would sure be pleased if he could have lived to see the day. . . .

175

It seemed a shame to break open the pretty gift parcels. She wasn't any good at making those clever bows or at wrapping things store-perfect. So many bright baubles. The warmth was opening the rose and drawing out its perfume. Some of the ladies never stopped talking. So many things to go on about to make the evening feel friendly, close. Poor grade five teacher, whoever she was, they were going to get up a petition and get rid of her. She didn't even mark all the spelling mistakes. Angela tore another wrapping and wondered with a little smile how many spelling mistakes in her box of pages. She tried to keep her mind on the presents and say the right things. How unreal. A popcorn maker. What was she doing here? She smiled politely into an electric frypan, watched the ribbon baubles collect in a riot of colours and twisting strands, smelled the rose opening to violence.

The faces all round were smiling, open with sentiment and kindness, as she opened the next fold of patterned bridal wrapping and kept her eyes steady on twin embroidered pillow-cases, HERS and HIS, pink and blue, with the rose wild under her senses. She kept her eyes down, not looking where the ooohs and the knowing little laughs came from.

"If only old Joe could have lived to see this day," somebody said.

"Poor old Joe, must have suffered."

Voices through the crumpling paper. Crumple it harder so you don't have to hear.

"But he sure did this community a service when he made the move to get rid of that Olson. Oh yes, didn't you know, it was him who got the petition started?"

Hold the hand steady. Smile at the gift. But keep the eyes down out of the eyes of the friendly faces. Oh Dad. My Dad. She breathed in hard on the rose.

The last gift, beautifully wrapped by the wife of the teacher who had come to take Mr. Olson's place. A card in the gift from both of them. They don't even know her. Three plaster ducks, each wrapped in white tissue, plaster ducks to fly across a wall. Father duck, mother duck, and baby duck. There's a tiny chip showing white on mother duck's mallard blue wing. Three ducks to put on the blue wall where her mother hung up the angels. This is ridiculous. What is she doing here? Oh

176

Mr. Moynahan, you were not my Dad at all. The faces come into clear focus, smiles for the bride, not for Angela. They don't know Angela. A silence has fallen among them and they are having to look too long at the girl who is taking the corsage from her shoulder and holding the yellow rose to her cheek.

Mrs. Ellis coughs with a little importance to ease the silence. The one with the accent laughs deep in her throat and jollies things along, calling "Speech."

Angela is taking the corsage apart, putting the pins and the metallic bow next to the ducks. Holding the rose to her chin. She looks into the faces and stands up.

Somebody claps, so everybody claps.

She is slow to begin, so they think she is shy and they smile encouragement. But this is more difficult than a valedictorian speech where you say what the faces want to hear. "Thank you for everything," she begins and she feels the warmth of their pride in the smiles upturned towards last year's valedictorian who is joining the ladies. She frowns a little. "Thank you for your love and the trouble you have taken." She is very dignified. "Would you forgive me and accept your gifts back." A little laugh trembles uncertainly round the mouths. What will she say next? Dinah Moynahan's strange daughter standing so tall with a rose by her chin. "Please forgive me," she said again and smiled courteously into the conglomerate smile of the ladies. "I have decided not to marry Gordon, not to marry anybody at all, at least for a long time yet."

The roar of the furnace is suddenly loud in the silence.

"Thank you again. I am sorry."

Then with the rose in her hand she picked up her beautiful furred funeral coat and was gone from them. She heard the worried buzz of exclamations as she pulled her boots on in the wet-floored porch.

Then she accelerated away across the snow-filled night. Singing. Out of the drift. In focus.

Dinah laughed. She sat down on the arm of Joe's old chair and fell over backwards into the seat laughing, laughing till tears ran down her face and Angela laughed because her mother was so funny crying. Dinah kept laughing and saying, "Oh poor Gordon, oh dear, if it weren't for poor Gordon!"

Angela sobered up and explained with the tremulous voice

after tears and laughter that she'd called in at Kopecs' on the way home and talked to Gordon. She thought she'd persuaded him to think about getting a job up north. He needed to get away and see something else, anyway.

"I would love to have seen the faces," Dinah laughed and wiped away tears. "Wait till Damion hears. He'll think it's the joke of the year!"

Dinah said why didn't Angela travel with her and finish out her year in Europe. She knew she could arrange to have the farm looked after until they had decided what they wanted to do about it. Angela smiled at her mother and said she wasn't sure, in a way it was nice to be home. She told her about Sam Lubinkoff who would be coming west with his music and how she'd like to see him. She said she'd like to be home when Damion came back south too and see what his travels had done for him. "And there are so many things I want to write," she said. "You have your art, Mum. And I have to write." Dinah just smiled like somebody singing and Angela smiled back understanding that it was her mother who had tried to keep the cage doors open—for all of them. Her mother.

When she went to her room she took the box of her writing and untaped it, put a new sheet of paper in her typewriter and wrote for the girl in the pages. The girl ended her novel sitting by a window watching magpies acrobating on the fat she had taken from the slaughtered pig and hung on her mother's trees. Magpies, gleaming poems of power, lunging at the fat, devouring. The hyacinths were in bloom again on the girl's window ledge. She wrote, "I am home. Home free—by the window. This is my home. Can I survive it? Me. The me who wants to sing inside. Solitary song.

"Mr. Olson, thank you for my wings. I will never fly away from the cries or the songs or the uncertainties because—I am Angela."

She dated the page and added it to the end of the last chapter, and put the box back in the drawer with the things she could not throw away, and went to bed with the curtains open and the snow falling steadily at the window.